SHOOTING
MONARCHS

SHOOTING
MONARCHS

John Halliday

MARGARET K. McELDERRY BOOKS
New York • London • Toronto • Sydney • Singapore

Margaret K. McElderry Books
An imprint of Simon & Schuster Children's Publishing Division
1230 Avenue of the Americas
New York, NY 10020

Book design by Russell Gordon
The text for this book is set in Aldine 401.
Printed in the United States of America
2 4 6 8 10 9 7 5 3 1
Library of Congress Cataloging-in-Publication Data
Halliday, John.
Shooting monarchs / John Halliday.—1st ed.
p. cm.
Summary: Macy and Danny, two teenage boys who have both grown up under
difficult circumstances, turn out very differently—one becomes a hero, the other a
murderer.
ISBN 0-689-84338-0
[I. Mentally ill—Fiction. 2. Criminals—Fiction. 3. Physically handicapped—
Fiction.] I. Title.
PZ7.H1545 Sh 2003
[Fic]—dc21
2001044725

FIRST
EDITION

For Peggy

SHOOTING
MONARCHS

1

A Thanksgiving Turkey

HE WAS BORN during the Thanksgiving Day parade. His mother didn't want to miss seeing the big balloons, so she made the nurse haul a TV into the delivery room. While the boy entered the world, his mother stared at a gigantic inflated Snoopy bobbing across the TV screen.

"It's like a miracle," she exclaimed. The doctor and nurse just shook their heads, seeing she meant the balloon, not the baby.

"What name should we put on the birth certificate?" the nurse asked.

The mother continued looking at the TV and said, "Macys."

The nurse glanced at the TV and asked, "You mean you want to name him after a department store?"

"Is there something wrong with that?" the mother responded belligerently.

"I guess there's no law against it," the nurse said with a shrug, but when she filled out the paperwork, she decided to leave the "s" off.

To his mother, Macy was just another mistake. He was a reminder, like her smoking habit and lack of high school diploma, of bad choices she had made. "I never wanted you in the first place," she frequently told the baby, even before he was old enough to speak. But she never considered giving him away.

By the time Macy was six months old his mother was regularly going out on dates. She turned on the TV and left him in the house alone. When he learned to walk and attempted to follow her, she locked him in his room.

One day when Macy was three his mother and a new boyfriend went swimming in the river. She left Macy home. Since it looked like a nice day, she decided to leave him in the backyard.

The yard was just a square of dirt surrounded by a solid wood fence. In the center was a rusty swing set installed long ago by a previous resident.

"You can play here until I get back," Macy's mother said. "I'll just be gone a few hours." Then, to be sure he didn't follow her or wander off, she took the loose end of an old rope that was wrapped around the swing and tied it tightly to his ankle.

As she bent over him completing the knot Macy gently squeezed her ponytail.

"Don't mess my hair," she told him.

"I love you, Mommy," he said, repeating what he had heard other children say on TV. His mother just walked away.

"I'll be back soon," she called without turning.

For the first hour or so Macy played on the swing. The rhythmic rocking back and forth always calmed him. He liked looking up at the white clouds, imagining they were large animals, mostly rabbits. When he got bored, he twisted the swing as tightly as he could, so tight it felt like it would explode, and then he got dizzy as it swiftly unwound. He might have played on the swing all afternoon, but the seat was cracked and began to irritate his bottom. So he played in the dirt.

The dirt under the swing was hard. It had never been raked or watered or seeded. Macy's mother never spent time in the yard during daylight. Many nights, though, after Macy was asleep, she went out to the swing. Like her son, she found the movement soothing. She smoked and flicked the remains into the darkness. The result was a great circular reef of cigarette butts around the swing.

At the center of the circle Macy scratched the dirt with his fingernails and found that beneath the surface the dirt was a soft powder. He made a small pile of dirt. He pretended the pile was a mountain and sent his pointer finger hopping slowly up one side of the mountain and quickly down the other. When he tired of the mountain, he scooped it up and filtered the powder through his fingers.

Then a drop of rain landed on his hand. Macy stared at the drop and watched as it slowly made a line across his dirty hand and fell to the ground.

The sky above the yard had become dark with clouds. A drop landed in Macy's eye and another hit his cheek. Then the rain became steady. Macy hadn't had anything to drink for hours, so he closed his eyes, turned his face toward the sky, opened his mouth wide, and caught the drops until his thirst was satisfied.

But the rain didn't stop. The holes he had dug to build his mountain filled with muddy water. His clothes were soaked and he was cold. He crawled under the seat of the swing for protection as the rain became a downpour. Then, when night came, he curled up in the mud and shivered. He never cried.

Macy's mother got home late and cursed as she tried to untie the wet rope from Macy's ankle. She had been drinking. When they got into the house, she told Macy to put on some dry clothes and go to bed. Then she dropped onto the stained, cigarette-burned couch and fell asleep. Macy watched his mother lying facedown on the couch, her wet ponytail touching the vinyl floor.

It took Macy a long time to go to sleep, so he lay in the dark and listened to his mother snore in the next room. After that night Macy never told anyone he loved them, and he was forever afraid of the rain.

Macy never did well in school and he didn't make friends. Starting in kindergarten, other kids made fun of him because he was so quiet and shy. The criticism caused him to become more withdrawn. In third grade his teacher organized a Thanksgiving Day play.

"Some of you will dress like Pilgrims and some of you will be Indians," she told the class.

Macy raised his hand for the first time all year.

"Yes, Macy?" the teacher asked.

"I was born on Thanksgiving," he said softly, staring shyly at the top of his desk.

Before the teacher could respond, one of the boys yelled, "That's why you're such a turkey."

Everyone laughed. Except the teacher and Macy. After that the other kids always called him "Turkey."

Macy's teachers were concerned about his poor academic and social skills, but when they called to schedule meetings with his mother, she said she was too busy. All the years Macy was in school, she never met with even one of his teachers. By the end of middle school Macy had stopped going. What should have been Macy's first year in high school was spent in a state juvenile correctional facility, where he had been sent for shoplifting at a liquor store.

Macy enjoyed his first afternoon in juvie. It looked nice, with a television room and a gym. The state's food was better than he was used to at home. And the prison uniform, an orange shirt with matching pants, made Macy feel like he was going to be part of a group. That night in the bathroom he was attacked by one of the bigger boys and his nose was broken. When that boy was locked in solitary, another boy took his place and broke two of Macy's front teeth.

One of the guards, Officer Quinn, was the teacher at juvie. He had been teaching there for over twenty years. Every Friday afternoon he conducted what he called "Quinn's Quiz." He asked the boys questions about their schoolwork.

Quinn's questions were pretty easy. If they had been studying geography he asked questions like, "What's the capital of the United States?" If the topic was science, he might ask, "What happens to water when it freezes?" But when he got to Macy, the questions were never straight-forward. Quinn tormented Macy.

"Okay, Macy," he said, with a gleam in his eyes, "if a plane crashes right on the border between the United States and Canada, where would you bury the sur-vivors?"

All the boys snickered while Macy pondered the prob-lem, and they laughed when he suggested burying the perfectly healthy survivors in Canada.

"Why would you bury them there?" Quinn asked.

"Because that's where they were going," Macy responded hesitantly. Everyone laughed at him again.

Quinn always asked each boy three questions, and Macy always answered each of his incorrectly. "What's heavier, a pound of feathers or a pound of rocks? How many animals of each kind did the pope put on his ark? Who got buried in Grant's Tomb?"

Macy felt mortified when the boys laughed at him. After the first few weeks he gave up trying to answer. When Quinn asked his questions, Macy just responded, "I don't know."

But even then, Macy was embarrassed as the other boys commented on his mental abilities. "What a dope. He's really stupid," they said.

By the time Macy got out of juvie he had several scars as souvenirs, but the deepest wounds were from the weekly punishment of Quinn's quizzes.

The first place Macy went when he got out was a tattoo shop. He had a picture of the earth inscribed on his
right forearm. Under the earth Macy told the tattoo artist
to write SATAN RULES. But when people saw it, they
wondered if it was a philosophical statement or a fashion
one because it actually said SATIN RULES.

After getting the tattoo Macy stole a car and was
arrested again. The police officer who drove him back to
juvie looked at Macy in the rearview mirror and said,
"I've always thought corduroy rules."

The next time Macy got out of juvie, he went to a
pawnshop he had heard some of the boys talking about.
He bought a gun. The shop owner didn't ask for any
identification or paperwork, just cash. On his eighteenth
birthday Macy used the gun to steal a Thanksgiving
turkey from a small grocery store.

The store clerk, Mohammad Aziz, should have been
off that night, but he was filling in for his boss.
Mohammad had recently immigrated to the United
States with his wife and four children, and he welcomed
the opportunity to earn extra money. This one night of
work would pay for next week's celebration of his son's
tenth birthday. Mohammad had just deposited all the
cash register money in a night security box and was
preparing to close when Macy walked into the store.

Mohammad was uneasy when he saw Macy. There
was nothing extraordinary about Macy's size or clothing,
but his face revealed a history of violence. There were
several fresh scars, his nose was knocked off center like it

had been hit by a truck, and his front teeth were broken. His head was completely shaven to conform to the popular style at juvie. Macy liked the bald look because it was easy to maintain without the help of barbers. The confinement of barber chairs and being touched by people with scissors always made Macy feel uncomfortable.

Mohammad felt fear as Macy approached him holding a frozen turkey. There was something cold and uncaring about Macy's emotionless eyes. If it was true, as Mohammad had heard it said, that the eyes are windows to the soul, then Macy's soul was a barren place. Macy's eyes lacked any hint of feeling.

Macy dropped the turkey on the counter, showing he held a pistol. "I want money," he said.

"Please don't shoot me," Mohammad begged, and abruptly raised his hands as he had seen done on television.

The quick movement startled Macy. Then the same finger that years before had hopped over an imaginary mountain beneath the backyard swing pulled the pistol's trigger, and Mohammad was dead. Macy took the turkey and left the store. He was never convicted of that crime, he never reflected on it, and he never felt remorse. His only feeling was anger because he wanted money and only got a turkey.

A few months later Macy got a job delivering pizzas. Customers were often startled when they opened their doors and saw Macy standing there with his battered face, bald head, and pizza. After he delivered the pizza, customers locked their doors.

One night after work Macy tried to rob a convenience store, but just as he revealed his gun a police car drove up and Macy ran away. He was surprised when the police arrested him a few hours later. But it hadn't been too hard for the police to track him. During the attempted robbery he wore his pizza uniform showing exactly where he worked and a badge that said HI, MY NAME'S MACY. So he was sentenced to the state correctional facility for adults.

Macy was the youngest prisoner in the overcrowded jail and was frequently mistreated by the older men. But he never complained, and after one year he was paroled to make room for criminals who seemed more dangerous. No one knew Macy had murdered Mohammad Aziz. As Macy prepared to leave the prison, a guard told him, "See you soon." The guard had seen many young parolees returned to jail in need of additional correction.

On the day of his release Macy went straight to the city and stole an old car. It was a massive gray wreck, at least twenty-five years old, with a rusted hood and a wire clothes hanger where the antenna used to be. The car was so worthless, the owner had left the key in the ignition, hoping someone would take it. The owner never bothered to report it missing.

After that Macy went to the pawnshop, bought a gun, and drove away. He had no destination in mind. He just drove.

Then he met Maria Hernandez.

● ● ●

Macy and Maria were as opposite as two people could be. Maria had been born to a loving family when Macy was three years old. Everyone said her parents were the perfect couple. They shared the same interests, including tennis in the summer and skiing in the winter. Mrs. Hernandez was a principal at one of the city's elementary schools, and her husband taught computer courses at the community college. Most people thought they had everything anyone could want. But they couldn't have a baby no matter how hard they tried.

One day while Mr. Hernandez was waiting in line at the supermarket, a mother in the next line was yelling at her small son for opening a box of chocolate cookies. She seized the boy by his shoulders and shook him so violently that the cookies spilled to the floor.

"Now look what you've done," she snarled.

Mr. Hernandez was always saddened when he saw a child with an abusive parent. It seemed unfair to him that people like that should have children while he and his wife had none. He opened a magazine to divert his attention, and his eyes fell on a large, two-page photograph of garlic. The headline across the top of the page read GARLIC, FOR BATS, BATTERS, AND BABIES.

The article said garlic was used for centuries to ward off vampires that appeared in the form of bats, and baseball players sometimes ate garlic to cure batting problems. The article concluded by saying, "It is also believed that garlic can bring on pregnancy. So be careful how you use it."

Mr. Hernandez tossed the magazine back on the rack, ran to the produce section, and loaded a bag with garlic.

"Have you gone insane?" his wife asked when she saw what he had bought.

"It's worth a try," he responded. "Babe Ruth said garlic helped him out of batting slumps."

"You're crazy," she said.

That night he added garlic to everything they had for dinner. He even put garlic in the vanilla ice cream.

"I'm not going to eat that," his wife complained, and she didn't.

Later that night while they were watching TV, he ate a whole garlic bulb as if it were an apple.

"You stink," his wife said with a laugh. "Don't get near me."

A month later they discovered she was pregnant.

They were delighted. But it wasn't an easy pregnancy. Six months into the pregnancy the doctor told Mrs. Hernandez she would have to leave her job and stay home. Continuing to work would jeopardize the lives of mother and baby. So she stayed home and was bored. The last three months of the pregnancy were the slowest months in her life. She couldn't wait for her labor to start, but when it finally did, it seemed it would never end. Twenty-three hours passed between the time they arrived at the hospital and the arrival of Maria.

"She was worth waiting for," Mr. Hernandez said. His wife agreed.

Maria was cute and smart and everybody liked her. Each year when her parents went to the elementary school, Maria's teachers would smile and ask, "What's the secret to raising such a great kid?"

"Garlic," her father always said, and the teachers gave him strange looks.

In middle school everyone discovered that in addition to Maria's other attributes she was fast. She could run faster than any girl who had attended her school. Her parents loved watching her run. Mr. Hernandez came to every one of her track meets and jumped and hollered every time she won. His enthusiasm was so outrageous that even the parents from opposing teams had to smile. Mrs. Hernandez attended most meets and quietly smiled at the performances of her husband and daughter.

By the time Maria left middle school, her name was atop half the lists of all-time records in girls' track-and-field events.

Maria was a little nervous about attending high school because it was a large school with kids from all over the city. She was sure that athletically and academically she would have stronger competition. She was a little worried about how well her talents would compare. But in high school Maria's body developed and she became even more athletic. She was slightly taller than average, thin, and had very strong legs. Every afternoon she ran several miles to the outskirts of the city and then walked and jogged home for dinner.

One of the reasons she liked running to the edge of the city was because there were still some small farms there among the encroaching housing developments. At one of the farms there was a beautiful brown horse with a white star between its eyes. The horse stood at its fence everyday as if waiting for Maria. When she got there, the horse raced along its side of the fence, and Maria ran as fast as she could on her side, enjoying the feel of her ponytail bouncing along behind her. At the end of the fence Maria always gave the horse a treat, usually an apple or a carrot, then she turned and walked and jogged home.

In her freshman and sophomore years of high school Maria won many athletic awards. Her parents sat proudly in the stands as their daughter received numerous trophies.

In Maria's junior year of high school the state track-and-field tournament was going to be held at her school. Mr. and Mrs. Hernandez felt this would be an opportunity for Maria to receive the statewide recognition they thought she deserved. They wanted everything to be perfect for their daughter, so they volunteered to paint the award platform. One Saturday afternoon a few weeks before the track meet they took cans of white paint and made the platform shine. On their way home they passed Maria on her daily run. Maria waved and her mother blew her a kiss.

Maria took her usual route away from the city. People who saw her that day later said everything looked normal. They didn't remember seeing anyone with her or near her. They didn't remember seeing any unusual vehicles.

Macy saw Maria and liked what he saw. He slowed down as he passed her, and she looked right at him, annoyed, because the fumes from his car's leaky exhaust bothered her breathing. She was relieved when he pulled away and the air finally cleared.

Maria wasn't surprised a little later when she saw the gray car parked ahead by the side of the road. The trunk was open, and she assumed the car had a flat tire or mechanical trouble. She didn't give it much thought at all, but as she tried to pass the car Macy quickly stepped in her path. He had the gun in his hand.

"Get in the trunk," he ordered.

Maria looked around in panic. She saw nobody. She considered screaming but assumed no one would hear her. She wished another car would come by, but the road was empty.

"Get in," Macy repeated coldly.

Maria climbed into the trunk of the car and Macy slammed the lid.

Macy drove away below the speed limit, carefully obeying the road signs, wanting to avoid being stopped for a traffic violation.

In the dark trunk Maria frantically felt for a latch or a tool or anything she could use to get out. As her eyes adjusted to the dark she realized a small amount of light was coming through a chink in the floor of the trunk. She pushed herself toward the hole and when she cleared away some damp magazines, she discovered the hole was large enough that she could fit several of her fingers into it. Maria looked through the hole and saw the pavement passing beneath.

Macy was looking for a place where he could take the girl. He passed the farm and the brown horse standing by its fence. He saw some new houses and decided to drive farther. He needed a place where no one would see him.

Maria began working at the hole. The floor of the trunk was rusted and she found she could use her fingernails to remove flakes of metal. Slowly the hole expanded.

Raindrops began hitting Macy's windshield. A few at first, then more, and he turned on the wipers.

Maria saw the pavement was wet. Then she felt the car slowing and the pavement turned to dirt. They had turned off the main road.

Macy didn't know where the dirt road led and he didn't care. He just knew that unmarked dirt roads usually offered seclusion. He drove a short distance and parked behind some bushes.

Maria was afraid the man would open the trunk. But he didn't. Macy wouldn't open the trunk until the rain stopped and that would not be until morning. He sat in the car looking at the windshield that was quickly fogged by his breath.

It rained all night. Maria could hear the rhythmic squeak of the car seat as Macy nervously rocked himself to sleep. When it finally became quiet, Maria began frantically peeling away bits of rusty metal. The hole grew slowly. She worked all night, and her fingers were bloodied from the work, but by morning she could fit just one arm through the hole. She felt the cool earth beneath the car. With her injured fingers, she slowly and deeply scratched her name in the dirt.

Then Macy opened the trunk.

A week later a family was leaving the city, and their kindergartner needed to go to the bathroom.

"There aren't any rest rooms along this road," the mother said, so they pulled off onto a dirt road.

"Look, Mommy," the child said, "it says something on the ground."

The mother saw the name and knew who it belonged to. Maria's disappearance had been big news the past few days. Behind some nearby bushes, facedown, the mother found Maria Hernandez.

The track meet went on as scheduled two weeks later. During the opening ceremony the school superintendent said they would dedicate the meet to Maria, and at the closing ceremony the principal said they would install a flagpole at the high school track as a permanent memorial to Maria. One of the boys on the track team wrote a song about Maria and sang it over the loudspeaker following the presentation of trophies. He said he wrote it especially for Maria's friends and family, but none of her family was there.

When the meet was over, Mr. and Mrs. Hernandez drove to the empty stadium. Mr. Hernandez carried a metal container. They walked to the center of the

stadium and stepped onto the sparkling white award platform. Mr. Hernandez opened the container and slowly
poured out the dust. Mrs. Hernandez held out her hand
and felt the dust that had been her perfect daughter filter
through her fingers.

2

Shiloh

LEAH AND SALLY HOFFMAN sat with their parents at the kitchen table. Sixteen-year-old Leah and her parents silently read the morning newspaper while nine-year-old Sally watched *The Price Is Right* and ate her cereal. Sally loved *The Price Is Right* and had watched it every morning for over a year. She liked other game shows too, but *The Price Is Right* was her favorite and inspired her obsession with prices. Sally wanted to know the price of everything.

"Dad, how much does a bottle of antacid cost?" she asked with milk and cereal dripping down her chin. A smiling lady on the TV was caressing a huge bottle of tablets.

"I have no idea what it costs," her father answered as he turned the page of the sports section.

A minute later Sally asked, "What did we pay for the gas barbecue?"

"About two hundred dollars," her father answered, sounding annoyed.

Sally was the only Hoffman who enjoyed talking at breakfast, and her early morning chatter had been irritating the rest of the family for years.

"Oh, that's terrible," Mrs. Hoffman exclaimed as she read the front section of the newspaper.

"What's the matter?" Mr. Hoffman asked casually.

"They found that missing girl, Maria Hernandez," Mrs. Hoffman said as she put down the paper and went to refill her coffee cup.

"Is she okay?" her husband asked.

"Unfortunately not," Mrs. Hoffman replied, and took a sip of coffee. "She's dead."

"You paid too much for the barbecue, Dad," Sally reported. "They just had the same one on *The Price Is Right* for a hundred eighty-nine."

"Sally, I think you're becoming a vidiot," her father said. "We're going to have to put a lock on the television." He had said exactly the same thing to Sally every morning since kindergarten.

"I'm glad we got out of that city," Mrs. Hoffman said. "It just isn't safe there."

The Hoffmans still read the city newspaper even though they didn't live there anymore. They had left the city five years earlier when they realized that, with computers, faxes, and overnight mail, they didn't need to live in the city to serve their city clients. With the latest technology, they could run their financial consulting business from almost anywhere. So they moved one hundred miles away to Shiloh.

The Hoffmans thought Shiloh was the most beautiful place on earth. It was set in a narrow valley between steep mountains that discouraged building and forestry. Some of the trees on the hills above Shiloh were the oldest in the state. The valley floor was fertile farming land that had supported local families for several generations. Farmers used most of the flatland for pasture and for planting corn, beans, and zucchini. Where the slope of the land became more extreme they planted fruit trees. Springtime in Shiloh smelled of fruit blossoms and freshly plowed earth. At harvest there was always an abundance of fresh fruit and vegetables, especially zucchini. Truckloads full of zucchini from Shiloh supplied supermarkets nationwide.

In contrast to its natural bounty, Shiloh lacked many of the basic trappings of civilization. Downtown Shiloh consisted of exactly five buildings. The general store, named "The Store," was in fact the only store.

It sold practical items, from apples to underwear, but as Mr. Hoffman frequently complained, "They sell everything you need and nothing you want." He missed the city's coffee shops and ice-cream parlors. The Store also served as Shiloh's post office. Doc Gumpass, Shiloh's postmaster and owner of The Store, located the postal service at the back of The Store so that everybody in town had to walk through rows of groceries, sporting equipment, school supplies, and hardware to get to their postboxes. Gumpass figured the inconvenient location of the postboxes was good for sales.

In addition to The Store, there were two churches in Shiloh—the stone church and the brick church—a garage for the volunteer fire department, and the sheriff's two-room office building. Sheriff Johnson was Shiloh's only law officer, and one of his main duties was directing traffic on Sunday mornings when both of Shiloh's churches got out at the same time. Originally there was one church in Shiloh, but when it needed a larger building, the congregation couldn't agree on the building material. Should it be stone or brick? After a decade of debate they decided to build one of each. There was no newspaper in Shiloh, no movie theater, and no fast-food restaurant.

But the Hoffmans were attracted by some of the things Shiloh lacked. There was no traffic in Shiloh, except on Sunday mornings. There were no crowds and there was little noise, except for Friday night football games at the high school two miles up the valley. And there was no crime. When everyone went to the football games, they left their houses unlocked. When people stopped at The Store, they left their keys in the ignition. No car was ever stolen in Shiloh. And there had never been a murder.

"I think Chad's coming," Leah Hoffman said as she got up from the kitchen table. The sound from Chad Peterson's old, green Toyota could be heard half a mile away.

"Can't he get that muffler fixed?" Mr. Hoffman complained. He wasn't fond of Chad.

"He likes the way it sounds," Leah said.

"It sounds more like a bulldozer than a car," Mrs. Hoffman said. She wasn't fond of Chad either.

"There was a muffler on *The Price Is Right* yesterday for only twenty-nine ninety-five," Sally said.

"Tell Chad, don't tell me," Leah said.

Leah had been dating Chad Peterson since they went to the Valentine's Day dance at school. For the three months since then, he had driven the Hoffman sisters to school every day. There were only two schools, the high school and the combined elementary and middle school, and they were right next to each other. Chad didn't like Sally, or any children, but he put up with her to please Leah. Dating Leah was very important to Chad because she was pretty, and he felt he deserved a pretty girlfriend. Leah didn't especially like Chad, but she needed a date for the junior prom, and she figured she could endure him until then.

Most people thought Leah Hoffman was the most beautiful girl in the valley. She was tall and thin with long black hair. She put her hair in a ponytail and poked it through the back of a baseball cap whenever she wanted to look athletic or casual, and when she wore her hair undone, she looked very mature and sophisticated. People frequently told Leah she should pursue a career in modeling.

Chad and Leah made an attractive couple. He was over six feet tall, with freckled skin and blond hair. He constantly worked out with weights to keep his muscles bulging through his clothing. He was quarterback on the high school football team and the best pitcher and hitter on the high school baseball team. His handsome looks and athletic abilities were useful tools in pursuit of his main goal in life: to be noticed. His success in sports, his bodybuilding, his dating Leah Hoffman, and even his noisy muffler were all aimed at attracting attention to himself: Chad Peterson.

"You could get a new muffler for about thirty bucks," Sally said as she got in the backseat of Chad's car.

Chad ignored Sally and leaned across the gearshift to kiss Leah. "Good morning, Gorgeous," he said.

Sally said the first thing that came to her mind. "Yuck."

The schools were located on the valley's main road, but Chad took a back road that was longer. It had less traffic and more curves, and Chad enjoyed speeding along it at twice the legal limit. Coming around a curve, Chad swerved and nearly hit someone walking beside the road. It was Danny Driscoll.

"Let's give him a ride," Leah said.

"No way," Chad replied.

"Danny's nice," Sally said.

"Come on, Chad, pull over," Leah told him.

Chad abruptly pulled off the road and stopped. "I should have run that freak over," he said.

Chad had never liked Danny. Chad resented the fact that Danny Driscoll was the best student Shiloh had ever seen. Chad and Danny had been in the same class throughout school, and every year when academic awards were given out, Danny always got most of them while Chad got none. Danny's SAT scores were almost double

Chad's, and everyone expected that after high school Danny would leave Shiloh for a big university. Everyone expected Chad would take over the family zucchini business, which was very successful and didn't require excessive brainpower.

Since they were little children Chad had ridiculed Danny's appearance. Danny was short and had no features that would be considered handsome. His hands and head seemed too big for the rest of his body, and his dull brown hair, which began thinning the first year of high school, looked like it would be completely gone by the time he graduated from whichever big university he would attend. His front teeth were so misaligned that at Shiloh's annual corn festival he could only eat corn by holding the cob firmly to his cheek and chewing with his side teeth. Worst of all, Danny had a birth defect that gave him an abnormal curvature of the spine. Before he was born, two of his vertebrae didn't develop correctly. The problem wasn't apparent when he was a baby, but by middle school he was noticeably lopsided and by high school he was obviously bent. "Congenital scoliosis" was the technical name for Danny's condition. It was a condition that could have been fixed with proper medical care, but Danny never went to a doctor. The Driscolls couldn't afford doctors. The result was that Danny walked awkwardly and looked as if his back were humped. Even on the sunniest of days, he walked with his head down, as if he were battling a cold wind.

Danny's spinal problem made many simple chores difficult. Overhead tasks, like changing a lightbulb or removing a book from a high shelf, were a burden. And ground-level jobs were hard too. Though his head leaned toward the ground, the rigidity of his spine made it a struggle to tie his shoes. Trimming his own toenails was almost impossible. So his nails became long and jagged.

"Look at his toes," Chad Peterson exclaimed in the school locker room.

As everyone looked at Danny's feet Chad said, "He's ugly from head to toe."

Leah Hoffman had never thought much about Danny Driscoll. Most of her thoughts were devoted to school and sports and dating. Danny seemed like a nice enough guy and she liked him, just as she liked almost everyone in Shiloh.

It appeared that Danny and Leah had little in common. Leah was a good student, much better than Chad, but her academic interests were not the same as Danny's. Danny's main interests were art, literature, history, and science. He was interested in almost everything, except mathematics. Danny wouldn't recognize a hypotenuse if one hit him on the nose.

Leah's only academic interest was math. She loved figuring answers to complicated math problems. On trips to the city with her parents she searched bookstores for books of math problems. Back at home, she spent hours in her bedroom computing the answers to complex questions in algebra, geometry, and trigonometry. Sally shared Leah's interest in numbers, and on one trip to the city they invented a game they called "Square Roots." One of them would choose a number and the other one had five seconds to identify the square root, give or take two tenths.

"What's the square root of 586?" Leah would ask.

"24.3," Sally would answer.

"Close enough," Leah would respond. "It's actually 24.2."

Then Sally would ask, "What's the square root of 951?" They played that game for hours and never got bored.

Danny Driscoll would need five minutes and a calculator to figure the square root of 4. Chad Peterson would have guessed a square root was a gardening problem.

Another thing Danny Driscoll and Leah Hoffman did not have in common was money. Leah's family was one of the wealthiest in the valley and Danny's was the poorest. The Hoffmans had new cars, a boat, stocks, bonds, and enough TV sets to make *The Price Is Right* accessible from every bedroom, the living room, the playroom, and the kitchen. The Driscolls didn't even have a bank account. When they needed a check to pay for something, Danny took cash to The Store and bought a money order.

Attendance at church also set Danny and Leah apart. Every Sunday morning Leah volunteered in the nursery at the brick church. Although the Hoffmans did not belong to the church, Leah enjoyed doing craft projects and playing games with preschoolers, especially math games.

Danny didn't go to church. His family had always belonged to the stone church, and he went there for a few years during elementary school. Every Sunday when they had a moment of silence for prayer, Danny prayed his back would be healed. He prayed outside of church, too. "Anything can be accomplished through prayer," the minister said. But as the curvature of Danny's back increased, his interest in church attendance decreased, and he eventually stopped going.

They had little in common, but Danny was infatuated with Leah from the first moment he saw her. Danny had secretly loved Leah Hoffman for almost five years, since the first day of seventh grade when she appeared at Shiloh Middle School. From the second Danny saw Leah, his life was changed forever. She was never far from his thoughts. In school he hoped they would be in all the same classes and be assigned the same projects. After school he invented excuses for walking by her house, and at night he often fantasized about saving her from life-threatening situations. In his fantasies Leah thought he was handsome. Sometimes in his dreams he had to die in order to save Leah, but as he lay dying she always kissed him; and for Danny, that made dying worthwhile.

In eighth grade every Thursday was "Formal Day." Everyone dressed up in their best clothes. Danny felt embarrassed by his clothes because they were all second-hand or homemade by his grandmother. So he got a part-time job at The Store to save money for new clothes. After a few months he got a ride to the mall in the city and spent all the money he had earned. He bought new shoes, a pink shirt, white pants, and a bright purple tie. The next Thursday he wore the outfit to school. Everybody told Danny how good he looked. Everybody except Chad Peterson. Before Danny got to class, Chad broke a pen and drained the blue ink on Danny's chair. Danny didn't see the ink, and by the end of class it had drenched the back of his new pants. When Danny realized what had happened, he went home. He never again dressed up for Formal Day.

In ninth grade Chad took his cruelest shot at Danny. They were in the same class studying Egypt. One day the teacher showed a videotape about Egypt that said the dromedary, or single-hump camel, is still used to carry cargo across the desert.

"Look," Chad said, pointing at the video of a dromedary, "it looks like Danny Driscoll."

Most of the class laughed, and before the teacher could restore order, Chad added, "That will be your new name, Danny. I'm calling you 'Danny Dromedary' from now on." And Chad stuck to his promise.

The teachers at Shiloh High School did not condone Chad's cruel behavior, but they were unaware of the extent of the harassment. Chad usually made sure teachers couldn't see his attacks on Danny. The few times the attacks were observed, Chad was reprimanded, but the teachers saw Chad's actions as isolated incidents rather than a destructive pattern of behavior.

In tenth-grade literature class they were studying the King Arthur stories. Literature was one of Chad's worst subjects. He never paid attention in class. One day he was being disruptive, and the teacher interrupted the class to ask, "Chad, could you please tell us what Camelot was?"

Chad thought for a moment and said, "I think it was a place to park camels." It seemed like a cute joke and everyone laughed. But then Chad turned to Danny and said, "That's where you should park, Danny." By the end of tenth grade Danny cringed whenever anyone mentioned camels.

At the beginning of eleventh grade the class studied marine mammals, and for a while Chad called Danny "Humpback Whale." After that Danny winced whenever anyone mentioned whales.

The relationship between Danny and Chad had been so negative for so long that Danny wasn't surprised when Chad nearly drove over him. A minute later Danny was skeptical when he realized Chad had pulled over to wait for him.

Sally Hoffman was watching Danny through the back window of the car as he worked his way toward them. Danny maintained a steady pace despite being loaded down with a backpack full of schoolbooks and a small suitcase holding a camera, extra lenses, film, and other photography equipment. Danny was the photographer for the high school newspaper.

Leah climbed halfway through the passenger-side window and waved back to Danny. "Come on, Danny, we'll give you a ride," she yelled.

Danny momentarily quickened his pace but had to slow down because he became short of breath. Danny noticed that in recent years, as his back problem worsened, his breathing had become more labored.

"He looks just like a camel," Chad muttered, looking in the rearview mirror and watching Danny hobbling toward them.

When Danny was a few feet from the car, Chad hit the accelerator and drove off. Leah nearly fell out the window.

"What are you doing?" Leah screamed.

"You didn't really expect me to allow that animal in my car, did you?"

"That's really mean," Leah told him. "Danny's a lot nicer than you are," she said as she buckled her seat belt and angrily folded her arms.

Danny stood alone in the road, the straps of his backpack cutting into his irregularly formed shoulders. He put his case of camera equipment on the ground, removed his backpack, and rubbed his shoulders. Looking at his shadow, crooked in the morning sunlight, Danny turned several ways, trying to make it look normal, but he failed. "Danny Dromedary," he said to himself.

Sally stared out the back window as Chad sped toward school. Danny Driscoll became smaller and smaller and eventually merged with all the beauty that was Shiloh.

3

Eddie Bauer

DANNY DRISCOLL ALWAYS got to school early. Even on days of heavy rain or two feet of snow, when parents throughout the valley let their kids stay home, Danny was among the first to arrive. So, despite Chad Peterson's lack of assistance, Danny trudged up the front steps of the school with plenty of time to spare. As Danny struggled through the heavy front doors of the high school with his books and camera equipment, Eddie Bauer's alarm clock was ringing two hundred miles away.

Eddie and Danny would never meet, but if Leah Hoffman were to create a graph to represent Macy's life of violence, they would both be on it. The line labeled MACY would descend through Mohammad Aziz and pierce Maria Hernandez. The same line would touch Eddie Bauer. Leah and Danny would be at the end of the line.

Eddie was a police officer. When he was growing up, he lived with his mother and his older sister, who were convinced Eddie would end up in jail. His life was on a dangerous course. His grades in school were mediocre, and outside of school Eddie and his friends often alleviated their boredom with petty thefts and vandalism. By high school Eddie was quickly drifting toward failure.

Eddie's life was turned around by a history teacher named Benjamin Rappaport. History was the only subject Eddie liked. He got C's and D's in everything else, but in history he usually got B's. Eddie had always been fascinated by the stories of earlier civilizations. The past seemed more exciting than the present, and he frequently dreamed of what his life might be like as an explorer with Lewis and Clark, a Revolutionary War soldier, or a pharaoh in ancient Egypt.

In Eddie's junior year of high school he was assigned to Mr. Rappaport's class. The teacher was new at Eddie's school, and everybody thought he looked funny. He was short and fat, and when Eddie first saw him, he thought the man resembled a short-legged bowling ball with a face. A leaky face, because the teacher's allergies caused constant dripping from his eyes and nose. Rappaport was new to teaching, but he was not young. Before becoming a teacher, he had spent twenty-five years as a tugboat captain. During all those years on the water he was never bothered by allergies, but on land he spent most of his time mopping his wet face.

When Rappaport decided to become a teacher, he told his friends, "I've been guiding ships for years, now I'll try guiding people."

Eddie didn't want guidance, and he thought the teacher was weird; but he liked Rappaport because of the way he immersed himself in historical roles. Whenever he talked about famous historical figures, he took on their characteristics. During the first day of class when he talked about

Alexander the Great, he turned his chair around and sat facing the class, waving a ruler wildly in the air, pretending he was going into battle on Alexander's favorite horse, Bucephalus. When he talked about Hannibal's daring invasion of Rome, riding elephants across the Pyrenees, he stacked several chairs on his desk and climbed dangerously atop, pretending his desk had become an elephant on a narrow mountain trail. And when he talked about Julius Caesar, he stood majestically on his desk, pretending he was riding in a chariot, reviewing his legions.

Eddie loved Rappaport's theatrics, and he loved the way he ended each performance. No matter whom the teacher was portraying, he ended the act by saying, "And he was short." According to Rappaport, every hero in human history was just about his height. Joan of Arc, short. Marco Polo, short. Napoleon, even shorter. After a year with Mr. Rappaport, covering thousands of years of history, many of his students were convinced all the world's accomplishments were attributable to short, fat people with runny noses.

Eddie wasn't short. In fact, he was one of the tallest boys in his class. But, since he liked Rappaport, he overlooked the teacher's favorable bias toward short people. Eddie didn't even object when, during a Civil War lesson, Rappaport asserted, "There is evidence to support the theory that Abraham Lincoln was a midget."

Halfway through the school year, Rappaport bought a new car. It was short and round, as if designed to resemble its owner. It was painted bright red.

"Look at Rappaport's new car," one of Eddie's friends said after school as they passed the teachers' parking lot. "Maybe we should take some of the shine off."

Eddie's friends didn't share his enthusiasm for history, or for the teacher.

"What do you mean?" Eddie asked.

His friend held up a sharp key. "I mean maybe we can scratch a message for him."

"Good idea," another boy agreed. "We can show him what we think of him."

"You just don't like him because you're failing his class," Eddie objected.

"So what?" the boy replied. "You just don't want to hurt his car because you're the teacher's pet."

Eddie's face reddened. "That's not true. I don't like him any more than you do," he lied.

The first boy handed Eddie the key. "Then let's see you do something to his car, Eddie."

Eddie took the key. "Okay," he said. "I'll do something, just to make you morons happy."

Eddie walked slowly toward the teacher's car while his friends backed away to a safe distance. Eddie didn't want to do any permanent damage. When he got to the car, he looked around to be sure no one was watching. Then he kneeled by the front of the car and used the key to release air from the tire valve. Air hissed as the tire quickly flattened. Then he began removing air from a back tire. As the car lowered to the ground a shadow fell over the tire.

"Is there something I can help you with?" Rappaport asked.

Eddie was caught, trapped. He slowly stood up. Over the teacher's head, he could see his friends running away.

Rappaport took Eddie's elbow and escorted him into the school. In the athletic department they found a bicycle pump. Then the teacher watched as Eddie reinflated the tires.

"Do you realize, Eddie, I could have you suspended from school, or maybe even expelled, for this?" Rappaport asked.

"I'm really sorry," Eddie said sincerely, continuing to pump. "I wish you wouldn't report this. My mother would be very upset."

The teacher was quiet for moment. "There's a school project I need help with," he said thoughtfully. "Come to my classroom next Monday afternoon, and I won't report this."

Eddie felt relieved.

When Eddie had completed inflating the tires and was walking away, Rappaport called, "Be sure to bring some old clothes with you on Monday."

The project Rappaport had in mind was rebuilding the school's sidewalk. Not just an ordinary sidewalk, but a sidewalk that would recount the entire history of the world.

As they stood outside the school on a cool, drizzly Monday afternoon, the teacher explained, "The sidewalk will be a time line. Every few inches will show important historical events. So as you walk along the sidewalk you will walk through history."

Eddie gazed down the long path where the old sidewalk had been removed. It extended for over three hundred feet. Rappaport's time line would be longer than a football field.

"The principal thought it was a great idea," the teacher concluded.

"What's my job going to be?" Eddie asked skeptically.

"You can mix and spread the concrete," Rappaport said. "Then, before each section of the sidewalk hardens, I'll etch a portion of the time line."

It was hard work. Eddie used a wheelbarrow to haul heavy bags of cement, sand, and stones to the front of the school. Then, in the same wheelbarrow, he mixed the three ingredients with water. When the mixture was the right consistency, he spread it between wooden frames to form the new sidewalk. As the concrete hardened, the teacher carefully etched dates and events. Every afternoon Eddie spent hours working on the project, and every afternoon the sidewalk expanded by only one small section. For the first few weeks Eddie trudged home tired every night, with aching muscles and concrete-covered clothes. But by the time they reached the construction of the Great Pyramids, Eddie was stronger. The work proceeded smoothly, and the teacher and student drifted into easy conversations about history, sports, movies, and the teacher's years as a tugboat captain.

Around the time Columbus sailed to America, Eddie realized the teacher's allergies had worsened. Rappaport began carrying a large box of tissues to absorb the floods from his eyes and nose.

"Eddie, what are you going to do after high school?" the teacher asked one day, wiping his nose with a tissue.

Eddie was surprised by the question. "I guess I never really thought about that," he admitted. The truth was, Eddie had avoided thinking about his future because it seemed so unpromising.

"Are you going to go to college?" Rappaport asked.

"I don't think my grades are good enough," Eddie said.

"Do you know what kind of work you'd like to do?"

"Not really."

The teacher took a moment to blow his nose. "Eddie, I want you to do me a favor. A friend of mine works over at the community college. She's in the career placement office." Rappaport wrote a name and address on a piece of paper. "I want you to go see her tomorrow. We can take a day off from the sidewalk. Tell her I want you to complete one of her occupation tests. I'll call to tell her you're coming."

Eddie didn't want to take any tests, but he didn't want to disappoint Mr. Rappaport. So he went to the college and took the test. When he saw the results, he was surprised. The test recommended he consider a career in police work.

"Do you think you'd like to be a police officer?" Rappaport asked when Eddie told him the results of the test.

"Yes," Eddie answered, with a smile, "I think I might like that."

"Then let's figure a plan," Rappaport said, wiping his nose again.

While Eddie mixed concrete for the settlement of the American colonies, they talked about police work and Rappaport wrote down the steps to becoming a police officer. A month later they completed the sidewalk. In the final section the teacher etched a large question mark, indicating that the future is a mystery. Then, at the very end of the sidewalk, he etched "Bauer & Rappaport."

Following the completion of the sidewalk Eddie became a better student. After high school graduation he attended community college. Then he transferred to a four-year college and eventually became a police officer.

On the police force Eddie endured a lot of teasing because he had the same name as a clothing store in a nearby mall. Eddie claimed they named the store after him since he had the name long before the mall was even built, but nobody believed him.

Eddie's wife, too, was often the target of good-natured jokes because her name was Edie. Edie Bauer, Eddie and Edie. She would have kept her unmarried name, but it was Meany, and she figured almost anything was better than Edie Meany. She would have married someone with a different name, but she loved Eddie Bauer more than she imagined it was possible to love anyone else.

Eddie worked from three o'clock to midnight at the police department and normally slept late in the mornings. But that day, the day Danny Driscoll was nearly run down by Chad Peterson, Eddie got out of bed early to finish a project before Edie got home from work. He wanted to surprise her by finishing the baby's bedroom. The baby was due in about three weeks. They didn't know if it was a boy or a girl. When people asked what they planned to name the baby they said, "Anything except Eddie or Edie." For months Edie had been asking Eddie to paint the other bedroom in their two-bedroom house. She didn't want to do it herself because the paint fumes might hurt the baby. But Eddie had never seemed to find the time he needed to do the job. Even after four years as a police officer, Eddie was surprised at how little time being a cop left for anything else. In addition to his normal shift on patrol, he had to do paperwork, make court appearances, and study for his master's degree so he could get promoted someday.

Eddie's spare time was also limited because of his many volunteer activities. As an adult, Eddie became one of the kindest people anyone ever met. He was always doing nice things for other people. In a way, he felt he was repaying the kindness that had been shown to him by Mr. Rappaport. If a charity needed someone to do door-to-door fundraising, Eddie would volunteer. Many weekend evenings he spent out at the rest stop on the interstate highway, giving away free coffee to weary travelers. At Christmastime he spent hours in front of the mall dressed as Santa Claus, ringing a bell to raise money for the poor. Recently, when another police officer lost her hair from cancer treatments, Eddie had convinced all the other officers to show their support. Because of Eddie, the whole police department was temporarily bald.

But this was the day Eddie would do something nice for his own family and finish the baby's room. Eddie skipped his usual shower and breakfast and drove straight to the hardware store. In less than an hour he was loaded with paint, rollers, brushes, and a wallpaper border with pictures of teddy bears, giraffes, and bunny rabbits. On the way home he stopped by the mall and bought colorful window curtains decorated with letters of the alphabet. Then he stopped by a furniture store to order a crib and a matching rocking chair. The supplies and furnishings cost more than he could afford, but Eddie thought it was worth the expense to see the surprised look on Edie's face when she came home from work.

Eddie started on the project as soon as he got home. The room was small and the painting went faster than he'd expected. He installed rods and hung the curtains. Then he carefully glued the wallpaper border along the top of each wall. Just as he was finishing his work the doorbell rang. It was the delivery from the furniture store. When the deliverymen left, Eddie fell into the new rocking chair and sighed with contentment. He was amazed at how much he had accomplished in such a short time. He still had a few minutes before Edie was due home from work, so he took his overdue shower.

When Eddie got out of the shower, he dressed in his police uniform. He always liked the way he looked in uniform. Whenever he saw himself in the mirror in his dark blue shirt and pants and the shoulder insignia that said in gold letters INTEGRITY, SERVICE, PRIDE he knew he had made the right career choice.

Eddie noticed there was a message on the answering machine. While he was in the shower Edie had called to say she had to work late. Edie often worked late. She was an emergency room nurse at the hospital and emergencies never seemed to conform to her schedule.

Eddie and Edie loved their jobs, loved each other, and loved comparing the gruesome details of their work. One night at a restaurant they were enthusiastically sharing stories, and the manager asked them to lower their voices. He said they were going to ruin the appetites of other customers.

They laughed about that on the way home. Eddie said, "Cops see a lot of weird stuff, but I don't know how you stand all the blood and guts at the hospital."

"Nurses are tougher than cops," Edie said, laughing. But then she was quiet, remembering for the millionth time that she wished her husband was not a police officer. The fact was that sometimes the blood and guts she saw in the emergency room belonged to cops. Her daily fear, a fear she never shared with Eddie, was that someday he would be her patient in the emergency room.

In her phone message Edie reminded Eddie that their eleven-year-old nephew, Justin, had an after-school soccer game. Eddie always routed his patrol by the soccer field whenever Justin had a game.

Before leaving the house, Eddie wrote a quick note to Edie and posted it on the refrigerator. The note said,

Don't go in the baby's room tonight. I love you.
Eddie.

There was no pressing business when Eddie got to work, so he headed straight to Justin's game. He knew he had already missed most of the first half of the game, but if there weren't any emergencies, he could watch a lot of the second half.

The soccer field was in a park near the middle school. The parking lot was separated from the field by trees and bushes.

When Eddie drove his patrol car into the parking lot, he saw an old, gray automobile parked in the far corner. It looked like someone was sleeping in the front seat. It was Macy. Eddie made a mental note to check on the car and its occupant if they were still there when he left the game.

The second half of the soccer game had just begun when Eddie got to the field. He was glad to see it was a 0–0 tie. Justin was the team's goalie and was never happy when the other team scored. Justin didn't really care if his own team scored or not because Justin viewed soccer as a competition between himself and the other team. Justin protected his goal from the opposing team like a mama bear protecting her cubs. Sometimes Justin growled as he ran to take the ball away from approaching opponents. The growling usually frightened other teams, and their coaches complained. But growling is allowed in soccer. Sometimes after Justin snatched the ball from an attacker, he barked like a dog. When his team scored a goal, Justin stood alone at his end of the field and howled like a wolf. Players on other teams often worried that Justin might bite them. On the soccer field Justin was pretty eccentric, but off the field he was a nice kid, and he and Eddie were best buddies.

While Eddie watched the game, Justin's team got a goal, and Justin howled and did a little dance. Then he saved several attempts by the other team and barked. Each time Justin made a save, the spectators, mostly parents, yelled with joy or frustration, depending on their loyalties. After Justin's third save Eddie looked at his watch and realized it was time to resume his patrol. He waved to Justin, but the fierce goalie was too preoccupied to notice.

As Eddie was getting into his patrol car he noticed the old, gray car was still parked in the far corner of the parking lot. He decided to investigate. He didn't expect to find a major criminal. Criminals, if they were successful, generally drove better cars than Macy's. From the looks of the vehicle, Eddie expected to find someone who was homeless, someone who lived out of their car, someone who might need assistance. He had encountered many people like that, and frequently he was able to help them by directing them to the food bank or the free clinic. In the trunk of his patrol car he kept brochures from many different social services agencies.

"I'm like the chamber of commerce for bums," he often joked.

It made Edie nervous that her husband became so involved with street people. "They could be dangerous," she warned.

"Most of them just need help," Eddie replied. "They end up on the street because they're emotionally disturbed or mentally ill. Sometimes their ingredients are a little out of balance. If you give some of them the right medicine or the right chemical, they'll act as normal as you or me."

"You think you're normal?" Edie laughed.

One of Eddie's favorite stories was about a street person he arrested for destruction of public property. Somehow the man had acquired a sledge hammer and used it to smash parking meters. He had destroyed twenty-five meters by the time Eddie caught up with him. Eddie encouraged the court to sentence him to hospital treatment rather than prison. The hospital found that the man responded so well to medication that he was released a year later and hired by the city. They gave him the job of emptying parking meters.

Eddie pulled up near Macy's car. Macy was asleep in the front seat but woke up when he heard Eddie's car door slam. He drowsily glanced out the car window and jolted awake when he saw the police car. Without looking down, he frantically began to feel around the floor under his feet. Macy assumed the police knew what he had done—the stolen car and the murder. He completely misunderstood Eddie's intentions. Eddie just wanted to be helpful. If they had a few minutes to talk, Eddie probably would have been amused by their similarities. Two bald men with the same names as stores. But they didn't talk.

Macy relaxed when he finally felt the cold metal of the gun. He slowly pulled it next to his right leg where the cop wouldn't see it.

Eddie signaled for Macy to roll down the car window.

Macy rolled down the window with his left hand. Any second now, he would swing his SATIN RULES tattooed arm toward the cop and put a bullet through his chest.

"Is everything okay, sir?" Eddie asked.

Macy didn't say a word. His grip tightened on the pistol, his finger on the trigger.

Just then there was loud cheering from the soccer field. Eddie looked toward the field and then looked back at Macy. "I want to help you and I'll be right back," he said quickly. "Don't go away." Then he bolted toward the field.

When Eddie got to the field, everyone told him that Justin saved another goal. Eddie waved at Justin. Justin was still barking, but he saw Eddie and waved back. Justin would never know that his biggest save that day was in the parking lot. By the time his uncle Eddie ran back to the parking lot, Macy was gone.

Eddie frowned as he looked for the old car. He thought the driver might benefit from a few brochures.

Eddie worked late that night. He didn't get in until

2:00 A.M. When he got home, Edie was in the living room, asleep on the couch. Eddie gently wakened his wife by resting his head on her belly. He liked feeling the baby's movements against his cheek. Then he made Edie close her eyes as they went into the baby's room. When he told her to look, she was astonished by what a lovely job Eddie had done.

Then they both sat in the rocking chair, Edie on Eddie's lap. They were tired from a long day, and in a few hours Edie would have to start getting ready for her job at the hospital.

With her hands on her tummy, Edie said, "We sure are lucky."

Mr. Rappaport never learned what became of Eddie Bauer because after just one year of teaching he returned to the allergy-free world of tugboats. He never knew that he guided at least one student to success. Once in a while Eddie thought of contacting the teacher, but he wasn't sure if Rappaport wanted to hear from a boy who had given him two flat tires. To Eddie Bauer, Mr. Rappaport would always be a hero. And he was short.

4

Danny Dromedary

"HOW MUCH IS the tomato juice, Danny?" It was Saturday afternoon and Sally was helping Danny Driscoll at The Store. All the merchandise at The Store was priced the old-fashioned way, with a black crayon. There were no bar-code readers or laser scanners at The Store. Sally was marking prices as Danny unpacked The Store's weekly shipment from the city. Bent over the large delivery boxes, Danny looked almost normal. When Danny couldn't reach items deep in the boxes, Sally unpacked and Danny marked. They were a good team. Sally helped Danny every Saturday because she had nothing else to do. There were no Saturday afternoon game shows on TV in Shiloh, and Sally thought working at The Store was good training for her future. A future that she hoped would include an appearance on *The Price Is Right*.

"I forget what we charge for that, Sally. Go ask Doc Gumpass."

The Gumpass family had owned The Store for almost one hundred years. The current owner, Doc, was a bit of an oddball. One of his oddities was that he cluttered his business with testimonials. Whenever anyone needed anything after hours, Gumpass wrote a thank-you note to himself and had the customer sign it. The result was hundreds of notes in Doc's own handwriting taped to the walls, doors, and shelves, thanking Doc for opening on Thanksgiving to provide an emergency can of cranberry sauce, staying open late to supply candles for a late-night anniversary dinner, opening early to provide eggs for someone's Sunday breakfast, and so on. There was even a note from Mr. Hoffman thanking Doc for opening on Christmas, when he needed batteries for Sally's portable *The Price Is Right* video game. Doc Gumpass liked to make a big deal of these emergency services, but the fact was that he lived alone directly above the store, so the emergencies caused him no great inconvenience. One time he opened The Store at 3:00 A.M. to provide a bottle of cough medicine for a sick child. The child's parent jokingly called him "Doc." After that Gumpass insisted everyone call him "Doc," even though his limited education left him about fifteen years short of earning that title.

When Sally found Doc Gumpass, he was in the basement methodically removing the foil wrapping from chocolate Christmas bells and scratching lines in the bells with his thumbnail.

"What are you doing, Doc?" Sally asked.

"I overstocked on Christmas chocolate, so I'm planning to sell these for the Fourth of July." He held out one of the scratched bells. "See, now it's a Liberty Bell."

Sally felt a little queasy as she looked at Doc's chocolate-covered thumb. "Doc, what price should I put on the tomato juice?"

"I don't know, talk to Danny," he replied as he unwrapped another chocolate.

Walking back upstairs, Sally guessed that part of the reason for the business success of the Gumpass family was that they hired people smarter than themselves. People like Danny Driscoll.

"What did Doc Gumpass tell you?" Danny asked.

"He told me to talk to you."

Danny thought for a moment. "Well, Sally, if you were on *The Price Is Right* and they asked you how much a big bottle of tomato juice like that costs, what would you say?"

"Two ninety-eight," Sally immediately replied.

"Then that's what we'll charge," Danny said without hesitation.

Sally smiled and happily marked the bottles. "I really like working with you, Danny," Sally said. Then she started pricing bags of marshmallows.

"I like working with you, too," Danny said.

"Could I ask you a question, Danny?"

"Sure, what is it?" Danny asked as he bent over another cardboard box of grocery items.

"Do you like my sister?"

Danny stopped what he was doing and looked at Sally. "What did you say?"

"I asked if you like my sister."

Danny could feel himself blushing and thought how ridiculous he was to be embarrassed by a child's simple question. "Of course I like Leah," he said, and in an effort to mask the strength of his feelings he added non-chalantly, "Doesn't everyone?"

But Sally wasn't easily misled. "I mean *like,*" Sally said with an exaggerated wink. She had been practicing her wink lately, in imitation of her favorite TV show host, but it wasn't yet perfected. Whenever she winked, her mouth dropped open, giving the impression she had been poked in the eye.

"Do you think Leah likes me?" Danny asked, trying to change the focus, not the subject, of the conversation. Danny began unpacking boxes of cereal, trying to hide his reddening face as he anxiously awaited Sally's reply.

"I know Leah likes you," Sally said with certainty. Danny took a deep breath.

"How do you know?" he asked.

"Because she said so that day when Chad wouldn't give you a ride to school."

"What did she say?"

"She said you're nice, a lot nicer than Chad."

"Well, I think Leah's nicer than Chad too," Danny said with a laugh.

"I wish *you* were Leah's boyfriend. If you like her, you should tell her," Sally said with finality.

"I'll think about it," Danny said.

"You think too much."

"Maybe you're right, Sally, but now it's my turn to ask a question."

"What do you want to know, Danny?"

"Ever since I met you, Sally, I've wondered one thing," Danny said, trying to look serious. "Why do you like *The Price Is Right*?"

Sally looked at him as if he had asked the dumbest question imaginable.

"I like it because it's good," she said.

"What makes it so good?"

Sally looked at the bag of marshmallows in her hand. Explaining TV to Danny would be like explaining a marshmallow to a Martian. He didn't have one, he didn't need one, and he probably wouldn't want one. But Sally decided to accept the challenge. "The show is good because it's exciting," she said.

"What makes it exciting?" Danny persisted.

"People win prizes. Don't you think prizes are fun?"

"It depends on what kinds of prizes," Danny teased.

"Oh, Danny, you should see the prizes they give away. Refrigerators, televisions, patio furniture, cars."

"Don't the people on the show already have those things?" he asked.

"Probably," she admitted in a defeated tone. Then she rallied and added, "But sometimes the prize is money."

"Money always makes a nice prize," Danny agreed. "I'd prefer money to patio furniture any day."

"What would you do if you won a pile of money?"

Danny paused. The first thing he thought of was getting his crooked back fixed. But he didn't want to say that. "I think I'd travel."

"Where would you go?"

"I'd follow the butterflies," he said. "Every year the monarch butterflies migrate to Mexico. From as far away as Canada, they fly up to fifty miles a day until they reach the Mexican mountains. They gather on the trees there. Sometimes the trees are so full of butterflies, the branches break and fall to the ground."

"Wow, I'd like to see that."

"So would I."

"But before you go to Mexico, you should tell Leah you like her," Sally said.

"I'll think about it," Danny said again.

"How much is the dishwasher detergent?" Sally asked, turning her attention to a small stack of unpriced boxes.

Danny was surprised that Sally's conversation was so upsetting to him. "She's just a kid," he told himself that night as he turned in bed, trying to fall asleep. All night he kept hearing Sally's advice: "If you like her, you should tell her." It seemed so simple. As Danny's bedroom began to lighten from the approaching dawn he got up to have breakfast with his grandmother.

Danny and his grandmother lived in the foothills outside of Shiloh. Their two-story house suffered from years of neglect. It was built by Danny's great-great grandfather and for generations had been surrounded by fruit trees. But since "the troubles," the house hadn't been maintained and the forest had overtaken much of the orchard.

"You're the only good that came from 'the troubles,'" Danny's grandmother told him.

"The troubles" was a period of about two years when Danny Driscoll's family had a lot of problems. "More problems than a possum has ticks," Danny's grandmother said. Danny wasn't exactly sure how his grandmother knew how many ticks the average opossum had, but he assumed it was plenty because "the troubles" had been a very hard time for his family.

"The troubles" started when Danny's mother was in high school. She was pregnant and in love with the boy, who promised to be supportive but left the valley a month before Danny's birth. He never returned.

"His leaving was a blessing," Danny's grandmother said. But that was the last blessing for a while because Danny arrived sooner than expected, while his mother was working in the orchard, and the birth had serious complications. Danny's mother lost too much blood before she could get medical care and she died. Danny's grandmother cradled the baby in her arms as she watched her daughter's burial in Shiloh Cemetery. Six months later Danny's grandmother suffered a stroke that weakened her left arm and leg. She never regained the use of her leg and was forced to use a wheelchair. After that she stayed in the house for months and delegated most of the child-care responsibilities to her husband, a man totally unsuited for practical pursuits such as diaper changing.

"He was the least practical man I ever knew," Danny's grandmother sometimes said, "but he was very sensitive. He was an artist."

The grandmother's medical problems took a lot of

money and prevented the Driscolls from having someone attend to Danny's spinal problem.

"We'll sell off a few acres to take care of little Danny's back," she told her husband.

But just as Danny's grandmother began to regain her strength there was a terrible accident. Danny's grandfather fell while trying to repair the barn roof. He died. "Losing your grandpa was a terrible blow," she told Danny.

So Danny's grandmother watched as her daughter and her husband were buried in Shiloh Cemetery the same year. Without her husband to manage the fruit harvest, Danny's grandmother failed to meet her debts and was forced to sell off most of their property. There was no money left for Danny's medical treatments.

Danny's childhood was solitary. He enjoyed school and hardly missed a day, but until he started working on the high school newspaper, he never participated in after-school activities. Everyday before school he helped his grandmother with breakfast and chores. After school he helped her with dinner and more chores. They didn't have a phone, a TV, or a computer, and his grandmother couldn't drive to the city, so Danny was never aware of the things that interested most other kids his age.

The reason Danny always helped prepare meals was that when he was about ten years old, he realized his grandmother was going to poison him. She wasn't trying to murder him; she was simply a very bad cook. Measurement was the problem. She never learned the difference between teaspoons and tablespoons, ounces and pints, and so everything was measured in pinches. Half a teaspoon equaled a pinch, a teaspoon was two pinches, a tablespoon was two big pinches, an ounce was four pinches, and beyond that, especially when she was dealing with liquids, things really got complicated and inaccurate. She measured the whole world in pinches and inches. The only fairly precise measurement she understood was the inch because she knew it was roughly half the size of her thumb. Later, as she aged, she lost her sense of taste. The result was that she served meat that smelled rotten and milk that was on the verge of becoming cheese. Motivated by an instinct for self-preservation, Danny developed an interest in cooking.

Danny's grandmother spent a lot of time reading. In all her life she hadn't spent a single night outside of Shiloh, so Danny assumed most of her wisdom came from books. Westerns were her favorite, and every Wednesday when the bookmobile came to Shiloh, Danny got her an armload of them. Danny liked reading too. He got piles of cookbooks and convinced his grandmother that she would be doing him a favor by letting him cook. Danny eventually discovered he enjoyed fixing food. By the time he reached high school he was preparing every meal at home.

The only kitchen job Danny's grandmother kept for herself was making dessert. She had a favorite recipe she called "gold nuggets." She claimed they were the favorite treat of prospectors, although as far as anyone knew, she had never actually met a prospector. Danny figured the gold nuggets were just an invention of some western novelist and meant only for fictional consumption. The dessert was made out of dry cereal, peanut butter, corn syrup, and innumerable pinches of sugar. The first Saturday of every month she mixed all the ingredients into a huge ball and broke off pieces that became "nuggets." Everyone who stopped by the Driscoll house was given a bag of nuggets to take home. Early in the month the dessert was gooey and tasted bad. By the end of the month it tasted even worse, and had hardened enough to break your teeth. Every night at dinner Danny pretended to eat the dessert while putting it in his pockets. Later he tossed the nuggets into the orchard, where he hoped they would not cause harm to innocent skunks, raccoons, and opossums.

Despite the gold nugget problem, Danny loved his grandmother. She was his best friend. And she truly loved her grandson. "Danny, I don't know what I'd do without you," she always told him. Whenever she reminisced about her husband, she used words like "strong," "brave," "sensitive," and "artistic." She told Danny, "You are a lot like your grandfather."

One piece of property Danny's grandmother did not sell during "the troubles" was her husband's camera. When she was young and healthy, she liked going with her husband into the hills above Shiloh to take pictures. His art was photography. Before entering the fruit business he had been a professional photographer, and he taught Danny's grandmother everything he knew. Before long she was displaying her best photographs in the meeting rooms of both churches. She alternated her exhibits between the churches to avoid any appearance of favoritism. Eventually, whenever anyone in the valley needed professional-quality photos of weddings, prized pumpkins, or new tractors, they called on Danny's grandmother. She said the worst thing about the stroke was that it kept her from taking her camera into the hills.

On Danny's eleventh birthday his grandmother gave him all the old photography equipment. In the morning she patiently taught him how to adjust the lenses and shutter speeds, and then in the afternoon, when she thought he was ready, she sent him into the hills to take pictures. When he got home that day, they rushed his film into the small darkroom off the kitchen and waited anxiously to see what developed. The first pictures Danny took of the mountain streams and wildflowers were beautiful.

"You've got a gift, Danny," his grandmother told him. "You're blessed with the ability to see the beauty in this world."

From then on, Danny frequently went to the hills to take pictures. It was peaceful there. School and work kept him from the hills most days. But every Sunday, rain or shine, while most of Shiloh was in church, Danny was in the hills. He liked taking pictures in the rain because he liked the gentle light and the way raindrops looked on leaves and flowers.

His favorite place to take pictures was in the high

meadow, where in spring and summer butterflies were attracted by the abundant flowers. Danny loved the contrast of the monarch's brilliant black and orange against the purple milkweed flowers.

At the school library Danny read about butterflies and learned that there was an extremely rare white monarch. Instead of orange and black, it was white and black. Every time he went to the hills, he hoped to see one.

After the sleepless night induced by Sally Hoffman's questioning, Danny had a quick breakfast with his grandmother, finished the chores, and headed out to take pictures. Danny's favorite time in the hills was early morning, when the rising sun illuminated leaves that still held dew from the night before. Spiderwebs that would be invisible to hikers in the harsh light of noon appeared for Danny as precious strands of jewels.

Danny's usual route into the hills was along a winding dirt road that eventually led to the high meadow. The road was originally established by the state to encourage logging above Shiloh, but environmental groups protested that idea, so the road was just used by occasional hikers and campers and Danny. Hardly anyone went into the hills around Shiloh, except for two weeks in late autumn, when hunters scoured the hills for deer. Almost everybody in Shiloh owned a rifle. According to Danny's grandmother, the first day of Shiloh's hunting season sounded like the gunfight at the OK Corral, Custer's Last Stand, or some other Old West mayhem, depending on which western she was reading at the time.

The forest was quiet as Danny trudged up the mountain road with his heavy case of camera equipment. The silence encouraged Danny to think. "You think too much," Sally had said. She was probably right. Sometimes he wished he could stop thinking. So many times he had come into the hills to take pictures and his thoughts were consumed, not by photography, but by Leah Hoffman.

There was a small clearing halfway up the road where campers sometimes parked their cars and pitched their tents. Ancient trees surrounded the clearing. Circles of charred rocks marked where visitors had their campfires. Danny always stopped there to rest. It looked like a peaceful spot, but often when Danny sat there, he was tormented by thoughts of Leah. When he was younger, he sat in the clearing thinking of strategies that would enable him to talk to her, ways to attract her attention, ways to show her how he felt toward her. As he got older he just wished he could leave his thoughts of Leah in the valley below. The worst time in the clearing had been right after Chad Peterson first called him "Danny Dromedary." That was back in ninth grade, and two years later he still hadn't recovered. It was the worst humiliation Danny had ever experienced, and it was made worse because Leah had heard it. For months after that, he continued his walks in the hills, but it was as if he were in a trance; during that whole time he never took one picture. Sitting alone in the woods, Danny still blushed whenever he thought of the devastating humiliation.

Danny realized he had allowed himself to become obsessed with Leah Hoffman. He knew her class schedule, he knew the books she liked, he knew her favorite bands, he knew she listened to Beethoven whenever she jogged, he even knew she had listed the names of her favorite professional ballplayers under the brim of her purple baseball cap. Danny knew his fixation on Leah was crazy. Sometimes he wished he could talk to a doctor about his obsession, but the only available doctor was Dr. Arnone, a traveling veterinarian who stopped in Shiloh once a week. Danny didn't want to discuss his problems with an animal doctor.

Danny's work on the school newspaper was just a means of getting close to Leah. She was on the school's cross-country team, and as the paper's photographer, Danny always covered their events, even though the team was horrible. They never won. Danny mostly ignored the other high school sports. The result was that in the Shiloh High School newspaper there were always photos of the cross-country team. Almost every photo included Leah Hoffman. When it wasn't cross-country season, the newspaper included Danny's photos of Leah's math team. Danny rarely took pictures of Chad Peterson's football and baseball teams, even though those teams usually won. When Danny was forced to photograph football and baseball, the pictures showed Chad striking out or scratching itchy parts of his anatomy.

Even Danny's job at The Store was partly motivated by his desire to see Leah. Certainly the Driscolls needed the money he earned, but another reason Danny willingly worked for the eccentric Doc Gumpass was that Leah regularly stopped by his business. Most Saturdays she came in for a can of cream soda while she was jogging. Nobody else in Shiloh liked cream soda, but Danny always made sure The Store had plenty of cold ones in stock.

It was during her brief stops at The Store that Danny picked up bits of information about Leah. "What music are you listening to?" "Read any good books lately?" Short questions, quick answers, then Leah would finish her soda and run.

Danny was certain Chad Peterson had no interest in Leah's musical or literary tastes. He felt it was unfair that Leah was with a guy who cared so little about her. Whenever Danny saw them together, his throat tightened and he became short of breath. When he saw them kiss, he wanted to die. He sometimes thought he would have been happier if he had been born blind, unable to see Leah and Chad. Sometimes late on Friday and Saturday nights he would lay in bed and hear the sound of Chad's faulty muffler echoing through the valley as he drove Leah home from a date. Then he would wish he were deaf, too, as he imagined where they had been and what they had done.

Danny's love for Leah was his great secret.

"If you like her, you should tell her." Sally's words kept repeating in his mind.

Easier said than done, Danny thought. *What if she laughs at me, what if she thinks I'm weird, what if she thinks I'm some sort of psycho?* Then Danny sighed, lifted his heavy camera equipment, and continued up the road.

The road ended at the high meadow. Not many campers made it this far because the road was badly eroded by years of runoff from rain and snow. The meadow itself, surrounded by low hills on three sides, was like a bowl that collected rainfall. There was a small pond near the center of the meadow that wasn't good for swimming or drinking water, but it was like a resort for mosquitoes, flies, and gnats. Campers who made it to the high meadow rarely stayed more than one night.

The bugs never bothered Danny because he always entered the meadow early, while the bugs were still sleeping off their nighttime frolics. Often when he got to the meadow, he saw deer silently drinking from the pond. On those mornings he would attach a long-distance lens to his camera and photograph the animals without disturbing them. Other mornings he quietly strolled through the long grass and wildflowers of the meadow, stopping for a few minutes to take a picture, the only sound the click of his camera. Sometimes he removed his shoes to walk through the meadow, enjoying the feel of the moist grass on his bare feet. As the sun warmed the meadow the butterflies began to appear. A few at first and then hundreds of them fluttered around Danny. He loved the butterflies and took more pictures of them than he did of Leah Hoffman.

The far side of the meadow ended at a fifty-foot-high wall of boulders. The wall was named "Shiloh Summit" and was the highest point on either side of the valley.

Danny rested his camera equipment on the ground and climbed to the peak of the summit. His climbing was awkward, but he proceeded steadily. From the top, Danny could see most of the valley. His shadow falling on the uneven rocks below looked straight and regular. He could see cars headed to the two churches far below him.

"If you like her, you should tell her," Danny said to himself. And at that moment he made a big decision. On the highest rock above Shiloh, standing as straight as he possibly could, he looked across the valley and yelled, *"I love you, Leah Hoffman, and I'm going to tell you so."* He was going to tell Leah how he felt, no matter what she or Chad Peterson or anyone else thought about it. And with that momentous decision behind him, Danny took a last look at the valley. It was still a beautiful day, but far to the south Danny could see a wall of dark gray clouds forming. It looked like someone was going to get a hard rain.

When he got home, his grandmother was in the kitchen reading one of her library books. She saw that Danny was in a happy mood.

"You're grinning like a mule eating briars," she said. "Did you get some good photos this morning?"

"Hardly any," he said as he began to prepare lunch.

"Then what are you smiling about?"

"I've made a big decision," he said as he put some meat in a pan on the stove. He was making enchiladas.

"What have you decided, Danny?"

"There's a girl I like at school. Her name's Leah Hoffman." Danny was surprised at how easily he divulged his secret to his grandmother.

"Is she part of that new family from the city?" To Danny's grandmother, anyone who had lived in the valley less than fifty years was new.

"That's right."

"She's really pretty, Danny," she said.

"How do you know?"

"She's the same girl I've seen in almost every single one of your newspaper pictures, isn't she?"

Danny blushed. "That's her. The problem is, I don't know how to talk to her."

"Afraid of rejection?" his grandmother asked.

"I guess so."

"That's natural. It's scary telling someone how you feel about them. I remember there was a boy in high school I wanted to go to the junior dance with in the worst way. His name was George Shifflet. And I remember that every time George came near me, my knees began to shake. Silly, isn't it?"

"So what happened?" Danny asked.

"I ended up going to the dance with Louie Gumpass, Doc's father. It was like torture trying to have a conversation with that boy. All night long he told me boring stories about his family's store. I learned more that night about the price of potatoes and the varieties of peas than any person should have to endure. You probably didn't know there are over a thousand kinds of peas. Of course, Louie's dead now. And he's probably boring everybody with pea stories in heaven."

"What happened to George Shifflet?"

"He didn't go to the dance. He probably spent the night sitting home. Maybe I should have asked him to the dance. Maybe he would have asked me, but he was too shy. I don't know. Maybe he would have been more boring than the Gumpass boy. In any case, he left Shiloh after high school and I never saw him again."

"So how did you meet Grandpa?"

"I first saw him at Louie Gumpass's wedding. The whole town was there, and your grandfather was there from the city because he was the photographer. Louie was the first one in Shiloh to hire a professional photographer for his wedding. All day long your grandfather was taking pictures of me instead of the wedding. Louie and his wife never did get any good pictures. After the wedding your grandfather stayed around Shiloh taking pictures, and I guess one thing led to another because we got married."

"I wish I could have known him," Danny said.

"I wish you could have too, Danny. He was a terrific man, even if he was no good at roof repair. But I'll tell you a funny thing, Danny. Even now, I sometimes wonder what ever became of George Shifflet."

"Maybe he wonders what happened to you, too," Danny said with a laugh.

"Maybe, Danny. But one thing's for sure: If you don't take that meat off the stove, you'll start a fire."

Danny quickly removed the sizzling meat from the

burner and turned the stove off. "Leah Hoffman already has a boyfriend," Danny said.

"Who is he?"

"Chad Peterson."

"I knew his grandparents. They made a lot of money growing zucchini, but they were idiots. Leah should be flattered that she's attractive to someone like you, someone with a brain."

"But Chad's handsome," Danny said as he continued to prepare the enchiladas.

"What's handsome?" his grandmother protested. "You're a photographer, Danny. You know that if your lens is slightly out of focus or if your shutter speed is set slightly too fast or too slow, you're not going to get a good picture. Just a tiny adjustment on your camera will make the difference between a great photograph and an ordinary picture. That's photography. Little things make the difference in people's looks, too. You know, Danny, an inch is only about the size of my thumb." Danny's grandmother held out her right thumb.

"So what does that have to do with Chad being handsome?" Danny asked.

"Everything," his grandmother said. "Take Chad Peterson and add an inch to his nose. Would Leah still think he was handsome? Add a few inches to his height, and people would say he's too tall; take a few inches away, and people would say he's too short. Move his eyes an inch farther apart or closer together, and see what people think. Handsome is just a matter of inches."

"I guess you're right," Danny said with a laugh, thinking of Chad with his eyes three inches apart. "But even if she thinks I'm an ugly toad, I plan to tell Leah Hoffman how I feel about her. And I'm going to do it this week. I don't want to be like you and George Shifflet."

"I might just try to track old George down one of these days," she said. "Maybe you'll come home from school someday and catch us necking." She grinned.

"Please, not while I'm eating, Grandma."

5

The Storm

THE DARK STORM clouds had been following Macy for hours, and every time he glanced in the rearview mirror, they were closer. He hoped to outrun them, but before he reached the city, he was overtaken. All the other cars put their headlights on to see in the darkness, even though it was only noon.

When Macy was in prison, he had liked to watch clouds. On nice days the guards let him go to an outdoor recreation area. Most of the other guys played basketball or jogged around the inside perimeter of the barbed-wire fence, but Macy just lay on a concrete picnic table with his arms forming a pillow behind his head and looked at the sky. He enjoyed playing his childhood game of imagining that the clouds were animals, people, and things. Sometimes the clouds would get gray, and then the guards would call everyone inside. It made Macy feel good that the guards didn't want anyone to get wet. One of the things Macy liked about prison was that when it was raining, he always had a roof over his head. He felt safe there.

Macy drove into the city just as the first raindrops hit his windshield. The old car's wipers were useless against the increasing rain. Macy couldn't see where he was going. He pulled off the main road and parked near a playground. Then he waited for the rain to stop.

But the rain didn't stop. Macy was going to experience the worst rainstorm in the city's history. Shiloh, a hundred miles north, was getting the same storm.

The first night of the storm, Sunday night, Macy sat alone in his car hoping the rain would go away. There were several leaks around the windows, so that by ten o'clock puddles had formed on the floor of the car. He pulled his feet from the floor to keep them dry. He ran the engine and heater to keep warm, but by midnight the car was nearly out of gas. So Macy turned the car off, held his knees to his chest, and shivered as he rocked back and forth.

There was more rain all day Monday and high winds. The heavy rain and absence of sunlight made it impossible for Macy to see what was happening outside. He listened to the car radio and got scared when the announcers talked about uprooted trees and downed power lines. He hoped his car wasn't near any of those things, but he couldn't be sure.

Late in the afternoon the radio said the rain would last another day, maybe two. Macy was tired, cold, and hungry. Rather then spend another frightening night parked near the playground, he decided to make his way to the downtown area. He hoped to find a homeless shelter. One night in juvie Macy had overheard two boys talking about shelters. "If you ever need a place to sleep in a city," one boy said, "you can usually find a shelter near the downtown bus station."

"That's right," the other boy agreed. "And if the shelter's full, you can always sack out on a bench and pretend you're waiting for a bus."

Macy nearly caused several accidents as he drove, almost blinded by the rain, to downtown. Fortunately, as he got farther into the city there was less traffic. Most businesses had sent their employees home early, and few people were venturing out for shopping, shows, or dinner. The downtown looked deserted. When Macy found the bus station, he drove around the block looking for the homeless shelter. He found it on the next street, just as the boys in juvie had predicted. Macy parked his car nearby and ran inside.

The shelter was run by one of the city's largest churches. The building had four floors. The top two floors were filled with bunk beds for homeless men. The second floor was for homeless women. Each of these floors had numerous showers and toilets at one end. Macy had slept in other shelters and noticed they always had more men than women, just like prison. The first floor of the building had a large cafeteria and a television room.

Tuesday morning it was still raining. Macy went downstairs for a quick breakfast, coffee and cereal, and then went back upstairs to his bed. He had no desire to socialize with the other residents. He sat on his bed, rocking and staring out a window. The rain cascading from the roof made him feel like he was sitting behind a waterfall.

At lunchtime Macy was pleased to see there was a hot meal. The volunteers were ladling chicken noodle soup into large Styrofoam bowls and loading paper plates with meat loaf and mashed potatoes. Macy took the soup and the meat and found a seat at a long folding table where no one else was sitting. He put his food down and went back quickly to get some milk. They had small cartons of white milk and chocolate milk. Macy took two cartons of each.

As Macy was enjoying his first "home-cooked" meal since prison, he became distracted as other residents sat at his table. One elderly man had an annoying habit of spitting into a plastic container he carried just for that purpose. Another man kept bending his head over the table and scratching his hair. Then he used his napkin to brush the dandruff, or whatever, away from himself toward the others at the table. Two teenage girls, one with purple hair and one with green hair, sat at the end of the table and spent most of their time giggling. Macy thought they looked weird. He didn't like the kind of people he saw at shelters.

Dinner at the shelter was spaghetti and meat sauce. Macy loved spaghetti but never liked the cheap, meatless sauce they served in prison. When everybody had their food, a woman wearing a red apron announced that it was time for the Lord's Prayer. Everybody stopped eating for a minute and prayed. Macy pretended to pray too, even though he didn't know the words. He figured prayer was a small price to pay for meat sauce. But Macy became uncomfortable when, following the prayer, the woman in the apron started walking around the cafeteria to talk to the diners. He finished his meal quickly and returned to his bunk.

The woman was Elizabeth Walsh, or "Reverend Betty," as everybody called her. It was Reverend Betty's job to keep the shelter running. She made sure sufficient food was donated to feed the homeless residents 365 days a year, she made sure there were volunteers every day to cook and clean, and she made sure there was enough money every month to pay the electric, gas, and water bills. Reverend Betty convinced doctors to volunteer their time so the residents could get basic medical screening every Monday morning. She found lawyers to give free legal counseling at lunchtime on Fridays. She didn't eat at the shelter, but five days each week Reverend Betty spent dinnertime there, helping in the kitchen and talking to the residents in an effort to meet their physical and spiritual needs. Then she went home to have dinner with her husband and their fifteen-year-old daughter, Jessie.

Betty had been running the shelter for a dozen years and was aware of almost everything that happened there. She knew most of the residents by name because they had been coming and going for years. She could usually tell who the new residents were as soon as she entered the cafeteria. Macy drew her attention immediately because of his scars and shaved head. She was sure she had never seen him before, and she hoped she would have a chance to talk with him. Feeding hungry bodies gave Betty the opportunity to save souls. When Macy abruptly left the cafeteria, she made a mental note to talk to him first if he returned the next night.

The storm continued on Wednesday. Macy spent most of the day in bed listening to the rain hammering against the roof. When he looked outside, he was frightened to see thick streams of dark water running down the streets. Clogged storm drains near the shelter caused one intersection to become completely flooded. As Macy watched, a car stalled midway through the intersection, and the driver needed to be rescued by firefighters. Macy was afraid the floodwaters would get up to the shelter.

Reverend Betty saw the anxiety in Macy's eyes when she sat across from him at dinner.

"Hi, I'm Elizabeth Walsh," she said, introducing herself. "Around here they call me 'Reverend Betty.'"

Macy just nodded and continued eating.

"How do you like the stew?" she asked. Every Wednesday night the shelter served beef stew.

"It's okay," Macy mumbled as he took another bite.

"What's your name?" Betty asked.

Macy looked up and stared at her a moment. "Joe."

"How do you like this weather, Joe?" she asked.

"I don't," he answered, and took a long drink from his milk carton. Then he wiped his sleeve across his mouth and took another bite of stew.

"I don't either," Betty said. "This storm's doing a lot of damage, hurting lots of people." Macy looked startled. "But don't worry, Joe," she said reassuringly, "there's nothing to worry about here."

"Okay," he replied. Then he quickly left the table, threw away the remains of his dinner, and walked upstairs.

The rain was less intense on Thursday, but city schools closed due to hazardous conditions. Several streams and a river overflowed their banks, causing severe flooding. There were power outages, and a few schools were struggling to repair roof leaks. The school superintendent announced that the city schools would be closed until Monday.

Elizabeth Walsh didn't like her daughter to be home alone, so she brought Jessie to the shelter to help prepare Thursday's dinner. Jessie was a sophomore in high school and had frequently helped at the shelter on weekends, holidays, and teacher workdays ever since middle school.

Dinner that night was one of Jessie's favorites, lasagna. While Macy was in line waiting for his food, Reverend Betty saw him.

"Joe," she called, walking toward him.

Macy didn't respond.

"Joe," she called again from a few feet away.

Macy turned and saw she was addressing him.

"Joe, save me a seat at your table tonight and I'll sit with you," she said with a smile.

That was just what Macy didn't want, so when he got to his table, he began shoveling the food into his mouth as fast as he could. It wasn't fast enough.

"How you doing today, Joe?" Reverend Betty asked, sitting down and patting Macy on his shoulder.

Macy flinched at her touch. "Okay," he responded, with a mouth full of lasagna.

"That's good," Betty said. Then she got straight to the point. She had learned through her years at the shelter that residents rarely stuck around long enough for the leisurely development of relationships. "Joe, the reason I wanted to sit with you tonight is that you seem like a man with a lot on his mind."

Macy didn't respond.

"It seems you don't like this storm we've been having. Most of us don't, but it seems like something else is bothering you."

Macy took a drink of milk.

"You know, Joe, I'm a minister, and I get to talk to lots of people who have made mistakes in their lives. We all make mistakes. Even ministers make mistakes. Maybe you haven't made any mistakes in your life, Joe, but if you have, you can be forgiven. Every night here we say the Lord's Prayer, which talks about forgiveness. Just keep in mind that Almighty God will forgive you if you ask. No matter what you've done."

Macy listened in silence and took another bite of lasagna. His eyes drifted up as someone approached them.

"Mom, I'm done in the kitchen." Jessie was standing across the table from them. Her red hair was pulled back in a ponytail.

"Just go and make sure everything's turned off," Betty instructed. "I'll be with you in a minute."

"Who was that?" Macy asked, following Jessie with his eyes.

"That's my daughter," Betty said as she stood up. "If you learn anything from your stay here, Joe," she concluded, "I hope you learn that God forgives."

The rain stopped.

Friday morning was sunny. Macy would have left the shelter, but he wanted to have one more dinner. He hoped to get another look at Jessie.

Macy was disappointed to see that the night's dinner was fish sticks. He didn't like fish. But his mood improved when he saw Jessie working in the kitchen. He ate his dinner slowly, hoping that Jessie would finish in the kitchen and come out. Reverend Betty saw him as he went for a second helping and decided to leave him alone. She had already delivered the message she wanted to give him. As Macy was getting his food he saw Jessie cleaning up in the kitchen.

Macy went back to his table and pushed his fish sticks around with his fork to give the appearance he was still eating. One by one the other residents finished their meals and went to the television room or upstairs. When there were only a few residents left in the cafeteria, one of the volunteers from the women's floor came down-stairs to get Reverend Betty. One of the showers was leaking, and the volunteer wasn't sure how to turn the water off. Within a few minutes, the other diners finished their meals and left Macy alone in the cafeteria.

Macy got up from his table and walked straight toward the kitchen. Jessie was the only one in there.

Jessie was wiping the kitchen counter and had her back to Macy. She had her favorite radio station playing and didn't hear Macy as he reached into the shelter's dinnerware to take a knife. He slipped the knife into his pocket as he approached Jessie. He looked around. They were still alone.

As Macy got closer to Jessie he could hear her humming along with the music. She was wearing a T-shirt and her hair was in a ponytail again. He stood watching her for a moment. He was close enough to touch her.

"Joe!" Reverend Betty yelled from the kitchen door. She never liked leaving any of her helpers alone, especially Jessie. As much as Betty believed in God's protection, she felt God expected people to take practical security precautions on their own.

Macy and Jessie turned toward Betty at the same time. Jessie was startled to see Macy so close. Betty walked to her daughter's side and put an arm around her shoulders.

"Joe, what are you doing in here?" she asked sternly.

Macy didn't say anything.

"Joe, I guess you'll be leaving the shelter tomorrow." It was a command, not a question.

Macy stood before them, looking at the floor.

"Do you have a car?" Betty asked.

Macy nodded his head.

"Do you know where you'll go?"

Macy didn't say anything.

"Well, where you go is up to you. But it's time for you to leave here," Betty said. Then, as a small kindness, she added, "Be careful if you head north. The storm washed out a bridge on the main highway. You'll have to go through Shiloh."

Macy turned and walked out through the empty cafeteria. On Saturday morning he left the shelter. He decided to go north, through Shiloh.

6

Abduction

SHILOH SUFFERED THE same storm as the city. School was canceled on Monday because there was no electricity. Whenever the weather did anything unusual—like too much rain, too much snow, too much wind, or too much ice—the power went out in Shiloh. During the storm Shiloh lost its power for ten hours. When the lights came back on, it was discovered that the roofs of both schools were leaking, so school was canceled on Tuesday. On Wednesday the roofers were still trying to fix the problems. By Thursday the four days of runoff from the hills was causing flooding, so just like in the city, the Shiloh schools were closed for the rest of the week. Most kids were happy about that until they learned a makeup week would be added to the school schedule in June.

By midweek Shiloh farmers kept from their fields and orchards by the heavy rain were gathering at The Store to get their mail and groceries and to grumble about the wet weather. The farmers lingered around The Store reading Doc Gumpass's testimonials because they had nowhere else to go, nothing else to do. Mr. and Mrs. Hoffman began lingering in The Store too because, without reliable power, their computers and fax machines were worthless. By the end of the week Doc Gumpass noticed The Store was running out of aspirin. He guessed everyone was getting headaches from being cooped up for so long. Danny theorized the headaches were brought on by too much reading of Gumpass's ridiculous notes.

Danny eagerly reported to work Saturday morning. He hadn't seen Leah all week, and he was hopeful she would come by The Store. Danny had lain awake the night before formulating a plan. Once Leah had bought her soda and was heading outside, he was going to say, "Leah, could I talk to you for a minute?" Then, on the front porch of The Store, he would reveal his feelings for her. He wasn't sure what would happen after that, and, surprisingly, he wasn't too worried. No matter what, he was certain he would feel relief from unloading the secret burden he had been carrying for so many years.

Sally arrived at The Store shortly after lunch and began unloading the weekly delivery from the city. There were more boxes than usual because The Store's shelves were nearly empty after the storm.

"How much is the aspirin?" Sally asked.

"Three ninety-eight," Danny said.

"It looks like they sent us about a thousand bottles," Sally said.

"We'll be ready for the next storm," Danny answered distractedly. He kept looking toward the door.

"Do you think we'll ever get another storm like that one?"

"Hard to say, Sally, but I hear we're due for more rain tonight." Danny looked up when he heard someone at the door, but it was just Doc Gumpass.

"Looks like more rain clouds coming up from the south," he announced cheerfully. Rain was good for business. "I'll be sitting out on the porch if you kids need me," he said.

Danny began revising his plan. He didn't want to reveal his innermost thoughts to Leah with Gumpass sitting there listening to every word. "I wish he'd watch for rain somewhere else," Danny grumbled to himself.

At the Hoffman house they weren't interested in rain; they were discussing the high school prom.

"Everybody's going to spend the night in the city," Leah repeated for the twentieth time.

"You're not," her father replied for the twentieth time.

"Leah, we're planning a perfectly safe, fun, non-alcoholic prom in the high school gymnasium. It'll be fun." Mrs. Hoffman was on the planning committee for the junior prom, but as the big night got closer it appeared that many of the students were planning a different kind of evening.

"Nobody wants to spend the night in a gym," Leah said, rolling her eyes.

"We have decorations planned, Leah. You won't even know it's the gym," her mother said.

"I'm spending the night in the city," Leah said.

"How are you going to get there?" her father asked.

"Chad," Leah answered.

"No way," Mr. Hoffman told her.

"Leah, it's not safe driving in the city," Mrs. Hoffman said. "Do you know how many high school kids die in car accidents on prom night?"

"No, how many?" Leah asked defiantly.

"A lot," her mother replied.

"That's right," Mr. Hoffman added. "You read about them every year in the newspaper."

"Well, Chad and I are spending prom night in the city with everybody else," Leah said with finality.

"That's what you think," Mr. Hoffman said.

"Are we done, Mom?" Leah asked. "I need to go for my jog."

"We can discuss the prom later," Mrs. Hoffman said.

It was just past 3:00 P.M. when Leah left the house. Her father later remembered the time because their argument about the prom made him miss the first few minutes of a basketball game on TV. Leah's jog that day followed the same route it always did. It was exactly one mile from their house to the main road and one mile along the main road to The Store. The round-trip always took less than forty-five minutes, including time for a soda at The Store.

At the same time Leah was leaving her house, Macy was approaching Shiloh. His eyes looked straight ahead; he did not see the beauty of the valley. He was tense. Ever since the storm he felt like he was getting all twisted up inside, like a swing that was twisted to the point where it needed to unravel. Several times he almost turned around to go back to the city and the shelter and that girl Jessie, but he decided that would be stupid. He was sure Reverend Betty would call the police. Then he saw Leah Hoffman.

Leah was wearing baggy shorts, a T-shirt, a purple baseball cap with her ponytail threaded through the back, and headphones connected to her CD player. When Macy saw her, she was just making the turn onto the main road. Macy slowed to take a good look as he passed. Leah didn't notice him. She was still thinking of the argument with her parents and trying to decide what she wanted. Sometimes she thought it would be more fun to stay home and play Square Roots with Sally than to go to the prom with Chad. Another car appeared behind Macy and forced him to speed up.

A quarter of a mile down the road Macy pulled over onto the grass. It was a pretty spot. On both sides of the road, cattle were quietly grazing on grass made lush by the rain. Toward the hills fruit trees were in bloom. But Macy felt uncomfortable. Just a half mile away, closer than Macy liked, was downtown Shiloh. Someone might see him from there. And there was traffic. Macy wasn't the only traveler taking the detour through Shiloh that day.

Macy knew he would have to work fast. He could see Leah quickly approaching on his side of the road. That was good. If she changed sides, he would have to leave her alone. She kept coming toward him. He walked to the back of his car and opened the trunk. Leah saw the car ahead but paid little attention. She was still thinking about the prom. When she was within a few feet of him, Macy showed her the gun and gestured toward the trunk.

"Get in," he said.

Leah was listening to her music and couldn't hear anything else, but it was clear what Macy wanted.

Macy looked around to see if anyone was watching. They were alone. "Get in," he repeated. Then he grabbed Leah and pushed her in the trunk.

Inside the trunk Leah quickly removed her headphones.

"If you make any noise, I'll kill you," she heard the man say.

Leah was terrified. She was also wet because the magazines and clothes in the trunk of Macy's old car were completely soaked from the storm. Leah began to shiver uncontrollably. But, surprising even to herself, Leah did not feel panic. Within seconds of being locked in the trunk, her mind was searching for ways to save herself, ways to solve the problem.

As Macy pulled back onto the main road Leah slid on the disintegrating magazines. Everything in the trunk seemed to move with her. Then she saw light. She saw the hole left by Maria Hernandez.

Driving through downtown Shiloh, Macy was tempted to stop at The Store. He was hungry. But he didn't want to take unnecessary chances, so he kept going. Doc Gumpass was sitting on the front porch watching the unusually heavy traffic and the approaching rain clouds. He later said he saw Macy drive by.

"Out of all the cars that drove by my store that day, his was the ugliest," Gumpass claimed.

Leah quickly pulled herself to the hole and breathed the fresh air. The pavement was passing underneath, but the car didn't seem to be going too fast. She reached through the hole and searched the underside of the car, trying to find the gasoline line or something else she could break to disable the car. Then Leah felt the car turn, and she saw dirt instead of pavement passing beneath her. Leah immediately knew where they were headed. There was only one dirt road so close to Shiloh. The road to the high meadow.

Macy was looking for a place to pull off the dirt road. He didn't want to drive too far, he just wanted a place where no one would see them. He was hoping the trees would provide some privacy. As he approached the forest raindrops started hitting the windshield. Macy stared straight ahead, hoping that if he ignored the raindrops, they might go away.

Leah had an idea. Before they reached the trees, she unplugged the headphones from her CD player and stuffed them through the hole. Seconds later she pushed her Beethoven disc through. Then the disc player. Then her baseball cap. Next she quickly removed a sneaker and pushed it through. Leah knew she could run barefoot if she had to. She was leaving a trail, and she hoped someone would find it. As she was working on removing the second sneaker in the cramped space, the car slowed. It pulled off the dirt road.

Macy had found the clearing among the old trees where campers sometimes stayed and where Danny had spent hours agonizing over his love for Leah. Macy turned off his car and waited for the rain to stop.

Leah wondered why nothing was happening. Perhaps the man was planning to hold her in the trunk until her parents paid a ransom. She heard the rain but had no idea that it was the reason her abductor stayed in the car.

Macy held his hands tightly over his ears. His legs were curled beneath him. In the trunk Leah felt the rhythmic movement of the car as Macy rocked back and forth. He wished someone would save him from the rain.

7

Late for Supper

AT 4:30 MRS. HOFFMAN said, "Leah should have been home by now."

"She probably needs time to blow off steam," Mr. Hoffman said, looking up from his basketball game.

"I guess you're right," his wife agreed.

At 5:00 Sally called from The Store to get a ride home. She didn't want to walk home in the rain. At 5:15 Sally was being driven home in her mother's car.

"Did Leah come into The Store today?" Mrs. Hoffman asked.

"No," Sally replied, "and I think it upset Danny Driscoll. He kept looking outside all afternoon, and he kept asking me if I thought Leah was coming today. I think he has a crush on her."

"That's nice," Mrs. Hoffman replied, but now she was worried. Where could her daughter be?

At 5:45 Mr. Hoffman said, "Don't worry, Leah will be home for dinner." The Hoffmans always ate precisely at 6:30.

"What if she's not?" Mrs. Hoffman asked.

"Then I guess we'll start calling around. She's got to be somewhere."

At 6:30 Mrs. Hoffman started calling Leah's girl-friends. No one had seen her all day. At 6:45 Mr. Hoffman called Chad's house. His mother said he wasn't home, he was camping.

"In the rain?" Mr. Hoffman exclaimed.

"You know how boys are," Chad's mother replied.

Mr. Hoffman never enjoyed camping, especially not in the rain, even when he was a boy.

"What do we do now?" Mrs. Hoffman asked.

"We'd better call the police," Mr. Hoffman said.

Leah had been locked in the trunk of Macy's car for more than three hours when the phone rang at the sheriff's office. The sheriff didn't hear the phone because he was taking target practice and wearing earplugs.

Sheriff Joseph Johnson had been in Shiloh for two years. He was a retired Marine and the only black man in town. For most of his twenty years in the Marine Corps, he did police work and saw lots of things he didn't like. He was frequently called in to handle domestic disputes. Sometimes he had to arrest fellow Marines for drug crimes. Occasionally he was involved in murder investigations. When he got out of the service, he wanted to stay in law enforcement, but he wanted to do it someplace peaceful. "I'm looking for a job with no hurries and no worries," he told friends and relatives. The position in Shiloh seemed perfect.

On his first day as sheriff, Johnson began converting the garage at his office into a firing range. He loved taking target practice with his pistols. It was a form of relaxation. It was also a source of pride because his aim was deadly accurate. He had a collection of pistols he'd gathered from around the world. His favorite one was from Italy. It had a mother-of-pearl handle. He had never lost a shooting competition with it. As much as Johnson liked his guns, he never wore one on duty in Shiloh. "I don't need a side arm to keep the church traffic in line," he liked to say.

Johnson had equipped his firing range with a visible signal to alert him to phone calls. So even though he couldn't hear the phone, he saw it was ringing. He removed his earplugs and went to his office.

"Sheriff Johnson here," he said.

Mr. Hoffman told him his daughter was missing.

"Sally or Leah?" Johnson asked. He knew nearly everyone in the valley.

Mr. Hoffman gave him some more information.

"I'll be right over," Johnson said.

Before leaving the office he called Veronica Allen. She was a math teacher at the high school and the only black woman in Shiloh. It was her first year at the school, and Johnson had been trying all school year to get a date with her. Finally she had phoned him because her cat was stuck up a tree. He almost told her that stuck cats were the fire department's responsibility. But he went to her house and saved her pet, and it resulted in an invitation to dinner. They were supposed to get together for dinner tonight.

"Hi, Veronica, this is Joseph," he said. "I have a little work to do, so I'll be late for dinner."

Danny Driscoll was just leaving The Store when Johnson started his car and sped off in the rain. Johnson's predecessor, Doc's cousin Early Gumpass, always bragged that during his twenty-five years in police work he never exceeded the speed limit. Danny wondered where the sheriff was going in such a hurry. Then he started the slow walk home in the rain, sad because another day had passed without telling Leah how he felt.

As Johnson drove toward the Hoffmans he reminded himself of the questions police are supposed to ask in missing-person situations. He had handled quite a few of these situations while he was in the Marines. Teenagers living with their families on the base frequently stayed out too late or sneaked off with friends in the middle of the night. Occasionally there would be a runaway. But in all his years as a Marine, Johnson never had a case where a child was abducted or harmed. They always turned up safe and sound. He had no reason to expect the Hoffman case would be different. No one had ever been abducted in Shiloh.

"When's the last time you saw Leah?" he asked the Hoffmans.

"She went out just after three o'clock."

"Did she say where she was going?"

"She was jogging to The Store."

"Do you know if she got there?"

"She didn't get there. Sally was helping out there this afternoon, and she didn't see Leah."

"Where's Sally?" Johnson asked.

"She's upstairs watching *The Price Is Right*."

"Isn't that on in the mornings?"

"She videotapes it."

"I should have known," Johnson said. Everybody knew of Sally Hoffman's fixation on that show. "Did you call any of Leah's friends?"

"We called all her friends. Nobody saw her."

"Does she have a boyfriend?"

"She's been seeing Chad Peterson," Mrs. Hoffman said.

"I've been meaning to talk to Chad about that muffler of his," Johnson said. "Did you call his house?"

"Yes, but his mother said he went camping."

"In the rain?" Johnson asked.

"It sounded strange to us too."

"Now, I don't want to get personal," Johnson said, "but has everything been okay at home? I mean, have there been any disagreements, or has Leah ever threatened to run away?"

"She's never talked about running away. But we did have a disagreement today about the prom. She wants to go to the city with Chad, and we want her to stay here."

"Did you resolve the disagreement?"

"It's resolved as far as I'm concerned," Mr. Hoffman said.

"Leah didn't feel it was resolved," Mrs. Hoffman added.

Johnson nodded. "I just have a couple more questions," he said. "Did you take a look around the house? There's no chance she's in the basement or up in the attic or watching TV with Sally, is there?"

"I looked all around," Mr. Hoffman said.

"You didn't see any notes or anything unusual in her bedroom?"

"Nothing."

"Well, Mr. and Mrs. Hoffman, I'm sure Leah will turn up. I'll put out a call to the other sheriffs' departments in the area just in case, and I'll check with some of her friends. I'll also check back with you in a few hours. In the meantime, if Leah comes home or if you get any new information, please give me a call."

Johnson wasn't worried as he left the Hoffman house. He was pretty certain he knew what had happened. It sounded like Leah had gotten angry at her parents and was spending the night with a friend, probably her boyfriend.

Johnson's first stop was Chad's house. Mrs. Peterson looked like a quiet woman, and when she answered the door, she was holding a wool sock she was knitting for her son. She verified what the Hoffmans had said, Chad was gone for the weekend. She said he was camping with some friends at a public campground twenty miles from town. Johnson figured he could drive out there after he had his dinner with Veronica.

The rain was heavier as he left the Peterson house. When he got to Veronica's at 8:30, he ran from his car to her door and was soaked by the time he got there.

"Go dry off," Veronica said. "I'll put dinner on the table."

As Johnson dried his hair in the bathroom he appreciated that Veronica didn't criticize him for being late.

Many women he had known never understood the unusual hours required by police work.

"Would you like a glass of wine?" Veronica asked as he walked into the kitchen.

"I would," he said, "but I'm still on duty." Then he told her the whole story about the Hoffmans and his theory about Leah's disappearance.

"I think you're wrong about Leah," Veronica told him. "I have her in my class, and she doesn't seem like the type of kid to do something like that. She really has a good head on her shoulders. She's about the best math student I've ever had."

"Plenty of girls sneak off with their boyfriends. It doesn't have anything to do with math," Johnson argued.

"I never sneaked off anywhere," Veronica said. "Did you ever do anything like that?"

"Why do you think I became a Marine?" Johnson said with a laugh.

"What do you mean?"

"When I got out of high school, my girlfriend and I went camping. She told her parents she was going with girlfriends. Unfortunately, her grandmother died that weekend. When her daddy came looking for her, there I was sitting in her tent. The next day I joined the Marines. I would've done anything to get away from that father of hers."

"I still think you're wrong about Leah," Veronica said.

"Then maybe you should come along with me later. I'm planning to drop in on Chad Peterson's campout. I'll bet she's there."

"I'll bet she's not."

"I'll tell you what, Veronica. If she's there, you'll have to fix me another dinner. If she's not there, I'll fix you dinner at my place."

"It's a deal," Veronica said, and they shook hands. On the way to the campground they both thought how clever they were. Whether Leah was there or not, they were guaranteed a second date.

It was a little after ten o'clock when they turned off the main road into the campground. By that time Leah had been locked in Macy's trunk for over six hours. The lights from Johnson's car illuminated empty campsites. Rain was pouring down.

"There's nobody here," Veronica said. "You'd have to be pretty stupid to camp in weather like this." But just then Johnson's headlights showed a car parked behind some trees. It was Chad's green Toyota.

"Bingo," Johnson said, and pulled into the campsite nearest Chad's car. "I don't see anybody. I guess we'll have to get out of the car."

"I'm not going out in that rain," Veronica told him.

"Don't worry, I have some rain gear in the trunk."

Covered in ponchos and equipped with flashlights, they walked through the rain.

"You're really a fun date," Veronica teased.

Chad's car was empty. Johnson removed the hood of his poncho so he could hear better.

"I think I hear something in the woods," Johnson said.

A short way into the woods they saw a light through the walls of a tent. As they approached the tent they heard voices and laughing. It sounded like a party.

Johnson used the butt of his flashlight to knock on one of the tent poles. "Open up. It's the police," he said.

Immediately there was a lot of movement in the tent, but no one said anything or unzipped the flap.

"Open up," Johnson repeated. "They're trying to hide Leah," he whispered to Veronica.

Chad eventually unzipped the tent, crawled onto the wet ground, and stood before his visitors. "Hi, Sheriff Johnson, is everything all right?" Then, surprised to see a teacher in the woods, in the rain, in the night, Chad said, "Hi, Ms. Allen."

"Who else is in your tent?" Johnson asked.

"Some friends," Chad said.

"Let's see," Johnson said.

Chad slowly pushed back the tent flaps. There were two other boys, friends of Chad's from school, and a pile of sleeping bags.

"Let's see what's under the sleeping bags, boys," the sheriff ordered.

Chad's friends reluctantly moved the sleeping bags. Underneath were several cases of beer with a few cans missing.

Sheriff Johnson sighed. "You fellows haven't been drinking, have you?" he asked.

The boys looked at one another. Chad broke the silence. "We had a few beers, Sheriff. But we're not doing any harm. It's not like we're out driving around or any-thing like that."

"Where did you get the beer?" Johnson asked.

Again the boys looked at each other. "We got it from our houses," Chad lied.

"So you're saying your mother gave you some of this beer, Chad?"

Chad didn't respond.

"When I was talking to her earlier this evening, she didn't strike me as the kind of mother who would give her son a load of beer and send him off for the weekend. I guess I misjudged her."

Chad was silent for a moment and then asked, "Why were you talking to my mother?"

"Because I'm looking for your girlfriend, Leah Hoffman."

"What do you mean?"

"She went out jogging this afternoon, and no one has seen her since. Have you seen her since three o'clock or so?"

"No, we left town around two."

"I hope you're not lying to me, Chad. You're in enough trouble as it is."

"I'm not lying, sir."

"Do you have any idea where Leah might be?" Johnson asked.

"No, I don't know where she could be. She didn't mention anything to me about going anywhere. I swear."

"Okay, I believe you," Johnson said, although he dis-trusted everything Chad said.

"You know, Sheriff, there's a guy back in town who's

obsessed with Leah," Chad said. "He practically stalks her. You should check with him."

"Who are you talking about?" Johnson asked.

"Danny Dromedary."

"Who?" Johnson exclaimed.

"Danny Driscoll, the guy who walks funny. He'd probably love to kidnap Leah."

"That's preposterous," Veronica said suddenly. She knew Danny well. He wasn't one of her best students, but he was one of the nicest. "I'm sure Danny Driscoll would never hurt anyone."

"I wouldn't be so sure," Chad said.

Johnson decided they had spent enough time with Chad. "Okay, boys," he said, "pick up all this beer and take it to my car."

When the beer was loaded in the trunk of Johnson's car, he said, "Don't even think of driving until daylight. If you move your car one foot tonight, I'll arrest all three of you."

"Looks like I owe you a dinner, Veronica," Johnson said as they headed back to town.

"Where do you think Leah could be?" she asked, looking into the darkness.

"She's probably home by now," he said hopefully.

When they got back to Veronica's house, Johnson used her phone to call the Hoffmans. They had no news about Leah. It was almost midnight, Leah had been in the trunk for eight hours, and for the first time since coming to Shiloh, Joseph Johnson was worried.

8

Cinderella's Sneaker

DANNY WENT RIGHT to sleep Saturday night. He was disappointed Leah hadn't come by The Store, but he felt sure he would talk to her soon. Soothed by the sound of the steady rain on the roof, he peacefully drifted off to sleep.

That night Danny had a vivid dream. He was in the high meadow. The colors were brilliant. He was setting up his camera for a shot of an orange and black monarch butterfly, but as he looked through the lens he realized the butterfly had changed from orange and black to white and black. It had become a rare white monarch. He stared at the unusual butterfly and thought how plain, yet beautiful, it was. Then he heard a noise behind him and turned to see Leah Hoffman running from the woods. She was being pursued by something wild, but he couldn't see what it was. He left his camera and ran straight and tall and fast to Leah's defense. In his dreams he was always swift and his back was never bent. He put himself between Leah and the thing. He battled the thing, and as Leah ran to safety he defeated it.

Danny awoke at dawn and prepared breakfast for his grandmother and himself. Then he gathered his photography equipment and walked toward the hills. The rain had turned to a light drizzle. Danny had seen days like this before. Animals in the high meadow didn't expect people on drizzly days, and their unsuspecting attitude had allowed Danny to get some of his best photographs.

Puddles in the road slowed Danny's progress. Some hikers would have merely jumped the puddles, but Danny, loaded with his equipment, was forced to go around. As he was approaching the line of trees that marked the beginning of the forest, he saw something in the middle of the road. It was a pair of wet headphones. They didn't appear broken. Danny assumed they had fallen from a hiker's backpack, even though it seemed odd that anyone other than himself would hike in such wet weather. Danny kept the headphones and continued up the road.

In the valley below, Sheriff Johnson was finishing his coffee and watching the clock. In five minutes, at 6:00 A.M., he planned to call the Hoffmans. He hoped their daughter had returned home during the night and her parents had been so relieved to see her that they had forgotten to call him. He knew that was unlikely, but it was possible. If Leah was still missing, he knew where he would have to look next. Danny Driscoll's.

While Johnson was calling the Hoffmans, Chad Peterson and his friends began breaking camp. The boys were subdued, thinking of the trouble they faced at home. They were sure Sheriff Johnson would report their beer drinking to their parents.

"Maybe everybody would take it easy on us if we were heroes," Chad said.

His friends didn't know what he was talking about.

"If we find Leah, I'll bet Johnson won't report us. I think on our way into town we should stop at Danny Dromedary's and see if he knows anything."

Chad's friends weren't in a hurry to get home, and doing a little detective work sounded like fun. They agreed to go along with Chad's suggestion.

As they loaded their gear in Chad's car he removed a long, slender bundle and said, "We don't want to cover this up. We may need it." It was Chad's rifle. He had it for target practice and hunting.

While Chad and his friends headed toward Shiloh, Danny continued up the mountain road and came to another large puddle. As he started to make his way around it he noticed something in the muddy water. Danny put down his camera equipment and got a stick to push away some of the mud. It was a compact disc. Fishing it out of the water, he saw it was a disc of music by Beethoven. Danny's heart began to beat faster as he wondered if the disc belonged to Leah. But he had never seen her jog on the mountain road.

Joseph Johnson was not surprised when he called the Hoffmans and heard they hadn't seen or heard from Leah. They were awake the entire night, and the loss of sleep had made them even more frantic. So now Johnson knew he had to visit the Driscoll boy. Veronica said she was sure he would never hurt anyone, but one thing

Johnson had learned in police work was that you could never be sure.

Danny's grandmother knew something was wrong as soon as she saw the sheriff's car drive up to her house. The police didn't pay social visits, especially first thing in the morning.

"Is Danny home?" Johnson asked.

"No, he's up in the hills taking pictures. Same as every Sunday."

"In the rain?" Johnson was beginning to think that every boy from Shiloh High School was out in the rain.

"He likes the rain. Nothing wrong with that, is there, Sheriff?" she asked defensively.

"Where does he usually go?" Johnson asked.

"High meadow," she answered. "What do you need Danny for?"

"One of his classmates, Leah Hoffman, didn't come home last night. I just wanted to see if Danny knew where she might be."

"I hope you don't think she spent the night with my Danny," his grandmother exclaimed.

"No, I'm not saying that," Johnson said. "I was just thinking, maybe she came by for a visit or something."

"The only Leah Hoffman we've seen around here are pictures of Leah Hoffman."

"What do you mean?" Johnson asked.

"Danny takes pictures for the school newspaper, and the Hoffman girl is on one of the teams. So we have a few photos of her."

"Could I see them?" Johnson asked. "If she doesn't turn up soon, I'll need pictures of her, and I'd prefer not to bother the family."

"Take a look in Danny's room; he probably has some there."

Johnson walked upstairs to Danny's bedroom. Since the grandmother was confined to her wheelchair, no one but Danny had been up there for years. Because the sun was not completely up yet, Danny's room was dark. The sheriff felt around the bedroom wall until he found a light switch. His first impression was how neat the room was, much neater than his own. Otherwise, the room looked completely normal. There were a few library books next to Danny's bed. All of them were about the migration of butterflies. One whole wall was covered with photographs Danny had taken in the hills, most of them of monarch butterflies. Johnson examined the pictures and was impressed by the obvious skill of the photographer. There was a small desk, where Danny kept his schoolwork, and a large dresser. Several boxes on the dresser were labeled PHOTOGRAPHS.

Johnson opened the top box. It held hundreds of photos. He reached in and took a few. The first one showed Leah Hoffman at a cross-country match. The second one showed Leah, apparently at the same event. The third was a close-up of Leah that Danny had taken with his long-distance lens. Johnson looked at a few more photos, and a few after that. They were all of Leah Hoffman. Johnson didn't like the look of that. As stupid as the

Peterson boy appeared, Johnson concluded he was right about one thing: Danny Driscoll was obsessed with Leah Hoffman. Johnson decided he needed to follow Danny into the hills. But first he would stop by his office. He wanted his gun.

As the sheriff was leaving the house Danny's grandmother called him back.

"I have a little something for you," she said, handing him a small paper bag filled with gold nuggets.

"Thank you, Mrs. Driscoll," the sheriff said, looking into the bag. When he got back to his car, he tossed the package onto the backseat. Though he had only been in Shiloh two years, he had heard hundreds of stories about the famous "nuggets."

Up in the hills Danny put the Beethoven disc in his camera case and tried to quicken his pace. Before he had gone much farther, he found the disc player. A few minutes later he saw a baseball cap in the road. He picked it up. It was soaked from being in the rain all night, but Danny immediately recognized it as Leah's. Under the brim was the smudged list of her favorite ballplayers.

Danny stood in the road holding Leah's cap. He was excited and scared. Excited that Leah might be nearby, scared that something must be terribly wrong. He shivered. "A rabbit ran over your grave," his grandmother always said whenever she saw him shiver.

Then Danny found one of Leah's sneakers.

9

The Rescue

SHERIFF JOHNSON HADN'T been gone more than fifteen minutes when Chad and his friends arrived at Danny's house.

"Where's Danny?" Chad asked abruptly.

Danny's grandmother knew who Chad was, and she wasn't going to be intimidated by him. "He's not home."

Chad decided to take a kinder approach. "Do you know where he is?" he asked politely. "We need to talk to him. It's important."

She wasn't going to be fooled. "Important for you or important for Danny?"

"Important for Danny," Chad said.

"Well, you boys can come back later. Danny's not home right now."

"He's probably up in the hills with his precious butterflies," one of the boys said derisively. Over the years everyone in Shiloh had seen some of Danny's butterfly photos at school art shows.

"Let's get out of here," Chad said.

Danny's grandmother watched as the boys disappeared up the mountain road.

• • •

In the hills Danny considered turning back to get help, but he decided to go as far as the clearing. He approached it cautiously. He was always fairly quiet as he walked along the road through the woods, but this time he was completely soundless. No one could have heard his approach. The clearing looked deserted. Danny thought the drizzle gave the clearing a dreamlike appearance. He walked a little way into the clearing and stopped. He saw Macy's gray car.

Danny crouched close to the ground and quietly placed his camera case beside him. He removed his camera and slowly attached a long-distance lens, then focused in on the automobile, which now appeared to be only inches away. It didn't look like anyone was in the car. He was going to walk toward the car to investigate when a movement caught his eye. There was something moving underneath. He gently adjusted the lens. A human arm was extended below the vehicle. It looked like the hand was scratching something in the wet ground.

By that time Leah had been in the trunk of Macy's car for over fourteen hours. She was wet and cold and tired. Macy had spent most of the night sleeping. Leah had heard him snoring and felt she was safe as long as he slept. While he was sleeping, Leah got ready for what might come next, preparing as hard as she would for a track meet or math test. She started by doing as much damage as she could. From inside the trunk, she disconnected the car's brake lights. She removed the rear lightbulbs and crushed them under the magazines. Then she gathered the sharpest pieces of glass to scratch Macy when he opened the trunk. In a corner of the trunk she found a rusty hubcap she could use as a weapon. As morning approached and she couldn't think of anything else to do, she decided to use a shard of glass to do one final thing. Like the city girl she had recently heard her mother talk about, Leah printed her name in the dirt. It was at that moment that Leah fully recognized the danger of her situation. When the trunk opened, she wouldn't be facing an athletic event or a test. And if her abductor was hoping for a ransom, why hadn't he phoned someone?

Leah continued to print her name. If anyone saw it, they would know she had been there. She was just completing the "n" in "Hoffman" when Danny spotted her. If he had arrived a minute later, he would have missed her. As Danny watched through his camera lens the arm retracted into the trunk.

Danny didn't know a lot about cars, but he knew arms didn't usually dangle underneath them. He also knew that cars had mirrors. So instead of approaching the car from the rear to investigate, he decided to circle around the clearing. He left his camera equipment on the ground where he had been. That was a mistake.

When Danny got around to where he could see the front of the car, he slowly moved toward it. The drizzle had stopped, and sunlight was beginning to filter into the clearing through the surrounding trees. When he was just a few feet from the car, he heard the sound of Macy snoring. Danny stopped and listened. Then he slowly went a little closer and peered through the side window. Macy was curled up on the front seat. He had an old shirt around his head. Danny guessed the shirt was to block out daylight, but Macy had wrapped it around himself to dull the sound of the rain.

Danny knew he had to move fast. He went to the back of the car and whispered, "Is somebody in there?"

Leah responded immediately, "Yes, please help me!"

"Is that you, Leah?" Danny asked.

"Yes. Who are you?"

"It's Danny," he said. "Danny Driscoll."

At that moment Leah and Danny heard the sound of a car coming up the mountain road. It was coming quickly.

"What's that noise?" Leah whispered.

"It's a car," Danny said.

It was Chad Peterson's car, the noisiest car in Shiloh. The sound woke Macy. Danny saw the bald head as Macy sat up. Danny promptly kneeled in the mud behind the trunk.

Macy rubbed his eyes and looked in the rearview mirror. Everything seemed okay. Seeing the rain had stopped, Macy got out of his car and stretched. Then he reached back into the car for his gun. Danny struggled to crawl under the car, but his back and shoulders wouldn't fit. He closed his eyes and held his breath as Macy walked by. Leah reached through the hole and held Danny's hand. Macy didn't see them.

Macy's mind wasn't completely clear. Sleeping in a car always made him feel dopey. He walked toward the road, where he could intercept the car. He didn't want any nosy campers getting near his car, so he would just tell them to go away. But if the loud car coming up the road turned out to be the police, he would shoot them. Macy tucked the gun in his pants as the car got closer. Then he ran to meet the car in the road. After a few steps he tripped over Danny's photography equipment. He looked at the camera, wondering how it got there. He was pretty sure he hadn't seen it when he drove in. Macy kicked the camera and it shattered against a rock. Then he went to meet Chad.

"There's one ugly face," Chad said to his friends as he rolled down the window of his Toyota.

Macy couldn't hear him. He was standing about twenty feet from the car and wasn't going any closer.

"We're looking for a girl," Chad announced. "Did you see any girls up here?"

"No," Macy answered.

"How about a guy with a hump on his back. He sort of looks like a camel," Chad said, laughing. "He would have been carrying a camera."

If Chad were smart, he wouldn't have said those things. If he were more perceptive, he would have seen Macy's eyes react when he mentioned the camera.

Macy knew he needed to act quickly.

"I think I saw the guy you want," Macy said. "He went by an hour ago."

"All right!" Chad exclaimed. "Which was he going?"

"That way," Macy said, pointing up the hill.

"Thanks a lot," Chad said. As they drove off Chad honked his horn and said to his friends, "That guy's face could give me nightmares."

Macy watched Chad's car disappear around the first turn. Then he ran back toward his own car. He knew that the camera guy was nearby.

While Macy was at the road, Leah and Danny took advantage of his absence, knowing they didn't have much time.

"He's gone," Danny said when he heard Macy talking to Chad.

"Get the keys," Leah whispered. "And hurry, Danny."

Danny struggled to his feet and found Macy's key in the ignition.

"Please hurry," Leah whispered as Danny tried to get the key in the lock.

In his nervousness Danny dropped the key into the mud.

"What's taking so long?" Leah whispered anxiously.

"Just a second," Danny said as he wiped the key against his pants to remove the dirt.

"Please, Danny, he'll be back any second," Leah pleaded.

Then Danny put the key in the lock and the trunk opened. Leah was flooded by fresh air and daylight. Danny was shocked by Leah's appearance. Her clothes and body were completely covered by ink from the wet magazines, she had cuts from the broken glass, and one hand was filthy from writing her name in the dirt.

"Here's your slipper, Cinderella," Danny whispered, removing Leah's sneaker from his jacket pocket.

Leah's muscles were stiff from her hours in captivity, but she was promptly out of the trunk and standing next to Danny.

"Go that way, Leah," Danny said, pointing toward a path away from the road. "That path circles back down to the dirt road."

Then they heard Chad's car horn.

"Hurry, Leah," Danny said, "I'll be right behind you. I'm just going to close the trunk and put the key back so he won't know you're gone."

As Danny quietly closed the car's trunk Leah disappeared down the path. Then Danny heard Macy running back toward the car.

Danny ran into the woods after Leah. He wasn't fast and he was soon gasping for breath. Macy ran into the woods behind him.

Leah had just reached the dirt road when she heard a gunshot. At the same moment Sheriff Johnson arrived in his patrol car.

"Help!" Leah cried as she ran to the car and collapsed onto the hood.

Johnson leaped from his car.

"Help Danny Driscoll," she cried. "He's still back there."

Johnson didn't need any more explanation because at that moment Macy raced from the woods. He was coming straight toward them with his gun in his hand.

Leah turned around and gasped. It was as if Macy were

approaching her in silent slow motion. His gun was pointed directly at her face. She felt frozen in place. As she stared at the approaching gun there was a loud explosion. Macy groaned as the gun flew from his hand and landed in the underbrush.

Leah turned toward Sheriff Johnson. His Italian pistol was pointed at Macy. Johnson had shot the gun right out of Macy's hand. Actually, Johnson's bullet had passed through the back of Macy's hand before hitting the gun. Macy moaned as he slowly sat down on the road, helplessly holding his mangled and bloody hand.

"Where's Danny?" Leah exclaimed as she ran past Macy and back into the woods.

Leah didn't see Danny at first. Then she heard a faint noise and found Danny lying on his back in a small patch of grass just off the path. Sunlight was streaming through the ancient trees.

It looked like he was resting, gazing at the blue sky above him. Leah ran to Danny. He had been shot.

Danny looked up at Leah. Even though Leah's face was smeared with dirt and ink from her long ordeal, Danny thought she was the most beautiful person he had ever seen.

"I love you, Leah Hoffman," Danny said softly.

Leah kneeled beside Danny and kissed him. Then, without a sound, Danny Driscoll died.

If the shot had gone only an inch in a different direction, Danny would have lived. But Macy's bullet had pierced his heart.

10

Memorial

SHERIFF JOHNSON LOCKED Macy in the back of the patrol car and quickly followed Leah. As soon as he saw Danny, he returned to his car and called for help, even though he knew it was too late. Then he went back in the woods and tried to console Leah. She was next to Danny and sobbing. Johnson put his arm around her and shook his head. If only he had arrived a few minutes sooner, he might have saved a life.

Chad and his friends soon came barreling back down the road and found Johnson and Leah in the woods. Chad looked at them and at Danny and immediately jumped to the wrong conclusion. "Nice shooting, Sheriff," he said.

Leah looked at Chad with horror and repulsion. That was the end of their relationship.

Later that morning Johnson drove Macy to the jail in the city. Sitting silently in the backseat, Macy saw the bag of gold nuggets. Handcuffed, and keeping an eye on the sheriff, he quietly ripped the bag. He bit into one of the nuggets and broke a tooth.

A week later newspeople from the city reported on the genuine sorrow expressed at Danny's memorial service, held in the high school gymnasium. Everyone in Shiloh was there, and everyone was sad. Sad about Danny and sad for his grandmother, but they were also sad for themselves. The town would never be the same. When people left their homes for the memorial service, they locked their doors. When they arrived at the high school parking lot, they locked their cars.

The first thing everyone saw when they entered the gymnasium were flowers. Members of the girls' track team had spent the whole morning gathering thousands of wildflowers from the hills around Shiloh. One of Danny's teachers and a few students from the school newspaper had put together collages of his photographs and displayed them on easels around the room.

When everyone was seated, the high school principal walked to the front of the room and stood behind a lectern. Members of the school's small band took seats behind him. Then the choirs of Shiloh's two churches entered from side doors and stood beside the band. The singers were wearing the robes they generally saved for Christmas and other special occasions.

The principal was the first to speak, and he said nice things about Danny. He was a good student, he had an excellent attendance record, and he never got in trouble. Then the band played a song.

The Shiloh High School band had never played at a memorial. Usually they played two concerts a year, winter and spring, and most of their songs were show tunes. There hadn't been time to learn any new songs, so they played something everybody knew. They played "America the Beautiful." They played it softly and slowly, and before they were done, many in the audience wiped away tears.

Next the choir from the stone church sang. "There will be peace in the valley," they sang, "no more sorrow, or sadness or trouble. There'll be peace in the valley for me."

The choir from the brick church sang another old hymn, but they sang only one verse. Over and over they sang, "Sometimes I feel like a motherless child, a long way from home." Each refrain was slower and sadder than the one before. By the time they finished, most of the people had bowed their heads in prayer or sorrow.

A few kids from Danny's English class read poems they had written for the occasion. Then the principal asked Leah to speak. Leah wanted the opportunity to speak, the opportunity to publicly acknowledge what Danny had sacrificed for her.

She looked thin and tired as she approached the lectern, but she felt strong. Leah was a good public speaker, and she knew what she wanted to say. She had spent a week gathering her thoughts about Danny and had made notes to help guide her through the short speech. But as she prepared to read her notes her eyes filled with tears and the words became blurred.

"I want to thank Danny Driscoll," Leah said. And that was as far as she got. She became overwhelmed by the emotions of the past days. Leah was sobbing. She tried to continue her speech, but it was impossible. Finally she rested her forehead on the lectern and cried.

Sally walked to the lectern and gently led her sister to an empty seat. Leah sat down, hiding her face in her hands. Then Sally returned to the lectern. It was too tall for her, so she borrowed a chair from the band. Sally stood on the chair and looked over the lectern at the audience.

"I was Danny's friend," she said. She told everyone about their Saturday afternoons together and how, through their hours of sometimes silly conversation, they formed a bond. She told them things some of them didn't know about Danny. How smart he was, how funny, and how much he loved butterflies.

"He was like the monarchs," Sally said. "They live short lives, too." Everyone could see Sally's eyes filling with tears, but she kept talking. She told the people about the monarchs, about how they often live no more than two weeks. "They come and go quietly," Sally said. "When we see them, it is only for a minute or two; but in that short time they remind us that the world is not a bad place. Bad things happen, but good things happen too. There are ugly things. Sometimes it seems there's a lot of ugly, but there's a lot of beauty if you look for it. Danny Driscoll was beautiful," Sally concluded. "He was like a butterfly."

Sally Hoffman knew Danny Driscoll as well as anyone ever would. In an innocent way Sally loved Danny. And he had loved her.

As the people were leaving the gymnasium something

happened in Shiloh that had never happened before. The choirs from the two churches came together. They softly sang an old Irish song: "Come ye back when summer's in the meadow, Or when the valley's hushed and white with snow, I'll be there in sunshine or in shadow, Oh Danny boy, oh Danny boy, I love you so."

A few weeks later Danny's grandmother gave his ashes to the Hoffman girls so they could scatter them from Shiloh Summit. "I think he'd like that," his grandmother said, her voice cracking.

Leah chose to skip the junior prom and picked that day to return to the mountain. As Danny's grandmother had requested, the Hoffman girls went together. Leah felt uncomfortable returning to the dirt road and expected to pass by the clearing without looking or stopping. But when she got there, she decided to go in and rest. Macy's car had been removed by then, and she was surprised that the scene of such frightening events could look so pretty and peaceful. She sat among the aged trees. A monarch butterfly floated by. She thought of Danny and regretted she hadn't known him better. But she felt honored he had loved her.

Before leaving the clearing Leah walked to where she thought Macy's car had been. She looked down. Her name was still etched in the ground. Leah fell to both knees and cried.

Moments later Sally walked to Leah's side and put a hand on her shoulder. "What's the square root of 735?"

Sally asked, bringing Leah's thoughts back to the present.

"That's easy," Leah said, standing up and wiping her eyes. "27.1."

The Hoffman sisters played Square Roots the rest of the way to the high meadow. It was a sunny day with a pleasant breeze and many wildflowers in bloom.

Leah and Sally stood on the highest rock at Shiloh Summit. Stretched below them was the beautiful valley, a sight Danny enjoyed many times before them. After several minutes of silence Leah opened the box. The sisters watched silently as Danny's ashes were carried off by a gentle breeze.

11

Justice

THE COURTHOUSE WAS one of the grandest buildings in the city. White marble steps led up to huge marble columns that surrounded large metal doors. Inside there was a tremendous lobby with more marble and an enormous glass dome that directed powerful beams of sunlight to the floor below. On sunny days some visitors stared up at the dome and felt like the intense sunbeams might draw them up to heaven. Others thought of hell as they loosened their collars in the uncomfortable heat. There was an inscription from the Bible in the marble wall just below the dome. It said, HE MAKES THE SUN RISE ON THE EVIL AND ON THE GOOD, AND SENDS RAIN ON THE JUST AND ON THE UNJUST. The part about rain might have made Macy feel nervous, but he never saw the lobby. People on trial usually came through a less extravagant side entrance.

Almost a year following Danny's murder, Macy was delivered to the courthouse in a windowless van. He was wearing handcuffs. He was taken upstairs in a plain steel elevator. He was locked in a concrete holding cell that contained nothing but a concrete bench and a TV. No one spoke to him.

The courtroom was crowded in anticipation of Macy's appearance. Like at a wedding, where guests sit on one side or the other of the aisle to symbolize their affinity to the bride or the groom, the crowd at Macy's trial squeezed into the benches behind the prosecuting attorney. Some people chose to stand rather than sit behind Macy's lawyer. No one in the room supported Macy. Everyone knew he was on trial for murder, and everyone knew he was guilty.

Macy's lawyer hoped the trial would end quickly. He had been appointed to defend Macy, just as he had been given the job of defending other criminals too poor to hire their own attorneys. But he had never handled a murder case, and he never had a client as clearly guilty as Macy. Guilty on two counts, because following Macy's capture the police had quickly tied him to the Hernandez murder. No one ever connected him to the murder of Mohammad Aziz. The lawyer believed in legal representation for all defendants, but he wished someone else had gotten this job. He felt embarrassed representing Macy. While waiting for his client, the lawyer tried to ignore the crowd by leafing through some real estate brochures.

Across the room the prosecuting attorney was full of enthusiasm. It was his first murder trial too, but it was just what he wanted. He always hoped his legal work would lead to a career in politics, and Macy was the perfect vehicle to carry him there. He had worked days, nights, and weekends preparing for Macy's trial. He was confident he would win a conviction. His only question was what punishment the jury would choose. His strategy was to overwhelm the jurors with evidence of Macy's brutality so they would sentence him to death. During the trial the prosecutor would tell the jury, "If this man doesn't deserve the death penalty, who does?"

When Macy was brought to stand before the judge, he looked up at the high courtroom ceiling, then he hung his head. He didn't want to see the judge, he didn't want to see the lawyers, he didn't want to see the people. He just wanted to get back to jail, where he felt safe. But when the judge insisted Macy raise his head, Macy glanced up and was surprised that he liked the way the judge looked. The judge was old, with white hair and a beard, and reminded Macy of Santa Claus.

"How do you plead?" the judge asked.

"Not guilty," Macy responded. Macy had always pleaded not guilty.

The trial was swift. There was plenty of evidence to prove he killed Danny, and there was substantial scientific evidence showing he murdered Maria Hernandez.

The first witness called by the prosecutor was Mr. Hernandez, Maria's father. Mr. Hernandez cried as he told the jury about his daughter. He frequently looked at the defendant, but Macy didn't look back. When Mr. Hernandez was done, the prosecutor called Mrs. Hernandez to the witness stand. She answered the few questions posed to her so softly that the jurors could barely hear her responses. They just watched as she cried and wiped tears from her eyes. When her testimony was completed, she joined her husband on a courtroom bench to watch the rest of the trial. They needed to see that justice was done.

The next witness was the medical examiner who had handled Maria's case. He described in detail what had been done to the girl. As he spoke the lights were dimmed and large photographs of Maria's body were shown on a screen at the front of the courtroom. The gruesome pictures and descriptions forced some people to leave the room.

Near the end of the trial Doc Gumpass was called as a witness. He had driven into the city and watched the whole trial with Danny's grandmother. After Danny's death Doc took a special interest in her. He ran errands for her, delivered her groceries, and drove out to check on her every few days, whether she wanted him to or not. He was regularly doing helpful things for her, and he never asked for a signed testimonial. As a witness, he didn't have much to add to the ton of evidence against Macy. But the prosecutor wanted him to say he saw Macy's car in Shiloh on the day of Danny's murder, so Gumpass gladly complied.

Leah Hoffman and Sheriff Johnson were the final witnesses. They told the jurors everything they knew about Macy. Leah described what happened and pointed directly at Macy when asked to identify her abductor. Johnson also pointed at Macy. Macy just stared at the table in front of him.

"Did the defendant show any remorse for what he did?" the prosecutor asked Johnson.

"No," the sheriff responded.

The jury wasted little time on Macy's case. The foreman of the jury was very efficient and businesslike and asked the jurors to vote on Macy's innocence or guilt before they had any discussion. The idea was to immediately find out how the jurors felt, how many thought he was innocent and how many guilty. The vote was unanimous; no one thought Macy was innocent.

The jury could have brought its verdict back in less than ten minutes, but the bailiff had ordered lunches. So, with their work quickly completed, the jurors enjoyed a leisurely lunch. News reports later said it took the jurors over an hour of deliberation to reach a verdict.

Macy just hung his head when the verdict was read. The judge scheduled Macy's sentencing for a few days later. There were only two options for Macy: life in prison or death. The judge who looked like Santa Claus wanted the jury to hear from the families of the victims before deciding which to give Macy.

On the day of Macy's sentencing Mr. and Mrs. Hernandez got up at their usual time and had breakfast in silence. During the year since their daughter's abduction they had essentially stopped talking to one another. They knew they shared the same thoughts, the same feelings, the same sorrows, and they saw no purpose in discussing them. Their interest in life was gone; they were just putting in their time. Before leaving for the courthouse, Mrs. Hernandez looked in the mirror. Whenever she saw herself, it amazed her that she looked so normal. Other than a few gray hairs, her appearance was unchanged from the last time she saw Maria. There was no physical indication that her heart was broken, her spirit crushed, her life ruined.

In her daily life, people at work, people in stores and restaurants, people who didn't know her would casually ask, "How are you?" She was always amazed to hear herself answer, "Fine."

At the sentencing hearing Mr. and Mrs. Hernandez were given the opportunity to speak. They stood before the judge and jury. Mr. Hernandez said what they both felt while his wife sobbed beside him. Several of the jurors cried too.

Mr. Hernandez said, "We came here today to tell you about our daughter, Maria." Mr. Hernandez could feel the tears welling in his eyes and wished he hadn't said her name. He took a moment to compose himself. "She was a beautiful child. She was"—he wiped his eyes— "she was the light of our life. I guess that sounds silly, but that's how we felt. And now that light has been extinguished.

"She was smart, she was athletic, she was beautiful. We can't express how much we loved her. Every day we think of her. Every hour. Every morning our first thoughts are of our daughter. We spend sleepless nights thinking of her. And we think of how she went out jogging one day, how she must have spent her last horrifying hours, and how we never saw her alive again. We didn't even get to say good-bye."

Mr. Hernandez paused and took a deep breath. When he resumed speaking, he sounded different. He sounded angry. "We think this man should be put to death," he said, and hit the table with his fist. He turned and looked at Macy. Macy was startled by the noise but kept looking down. Hernandez turned to face the jury. "Courts are supposed to aim for justice," he continued, and pounded the table again. "And for what is fair. But there can be no fairness for us in this case, no justice for us, because there is no punishment that can nearly match our loss." With each word, "fairness," "justice," and "punishment," he hit the table.

Mr. Hernandez took a moment to collect his thoughts. When he spoke again, it was without emotion. "No punishment for this man could be severe enough to give him what he deserves. He stole our little girl. He took her and he terrorized her. He assaulted her, he killed her. If you give him the death penalty, he will live in jail, probably for years, while there are endless legal motions and appeals. He'll be fed and clothed at taxpayers' expense, at our expense. If he gets sick, he'll be given medical care. If he has a toothache, he'll go to a dentist."

Mr. Hernandez paused to look at Macy. "He's sitting there hoping he'll get out of prison someday. Even if you sentence him to death, after years go by, he'll claim he didn't get a fair trial. He'll claim that you made a mistake. He'll claim he is innocent. And maybe he'll be set free to kill someone else's child."

Mr. Hernandez turned toward the jury. "But if all his delaying tactics are finally exhausted, what will happen? What will his ultimate punishment be? On his final day he'll be given a nice dinner, a chat with a minister, and then a quiet, institutional death. I wish our Maria could have lived so long; we wish she could have died so peacefully. For the sake of our daughter and for the sake of justice, you must put this evil man to death."

Several of the jurors nodded their heads in agreement as Mr. Hernandez led his wife back to their seats.

The only other speaker was Danny's grandmother. She felt that Danny would have wanted her to say something.

Doc Gumpass pushed her wheelchair to the front of the courtroom and stood behind her as she spoke to the judge and jury.

"My grandson, Danny, was a good boy," she said. "Sometimes I told him I didn't know how I'd live without him. But he's dead and I'm still living. At least I think I'm living because this sure doesn't look like heaven." Everyone nodded sympathetically, but as she tried to continue her jaw began to quiver. "I just hope Danny knew how much I loved him. I wish I had told him that more often."

With one hand, she turned her wheelchair to face Macy. "My Danny was peaceful," she continued. "He never did anything to harm anyone or anything. Sometimes other kids made fun of him and hurt his feelings. That was mean. People are mean sometimes. But to kill my Danny, well, that was just crazy." She was looking straight at Macy, but he turned his head away, still looking down. "Anybody who did what you did isn't right in the head," she said.

She turned her chair again to face the judge. "Danny didn't believe in violence, and I don't either. That's not our way. If Danny was killed by a wild animal, a bear or mountain lion, I'd say go ahead and kill it, make sure it doesn't do any more harm."

She paused and turned to face the jury. "To me, this man is like an animal. He sits here in this fancy building with judges and lawyers, but he's just like a wild animal." She turned to face Macy again. "But he's not an animal. I don't know why he did the things he's done. Maybe he's insane. Maybe people were mean to him like they sometimes were to my Danny. Maybe if somebody gave him just an inch of kindness, things would be different. I don't know."

She turned her chair toward the judge. "But I know one thing for sure: This man's not an animal. He's a person. Whether we like it or not, he's one of us, and we need to treat him with dignity. Because life is sacred, even if he doesn't know it. If we kill this man, it seems like we're saying killing is all right. But killing for killing just doesn't make sense."

She turned her chair to face Mr. and Mrs. Hernandez. "Killing this man will not bring my Danny back, or your daughter, either. There's nothing to be gained by hanging this poor soul, or pumping him full of poison, or doing whatever we do to kill people. I know killing him won't make me feel any better. Killing him wouldn't be something to be proud of. We all know he killed people. Let that be the end of it. Let's not continue the killing."

She turned her chair to face the jury again. "I'm certain my Danny would feel sorry if he knew you decided to take this man's life," she said.

Then she turned her chair and said, "Let's go home to Shiloh, Doc."

Moments later the judge gave final instructions to the jurors and sent them to the jury room to deliberate. Just as the jurors were preparing to vote on Macy's sentence, the bailiff entered the room.

The bailiff handed a bag to the foreman and said, "That lady in the wheelchair asked me to give you this."

It was a bag of gold nuggets. "These look good," the foreman said, looking into the bag. He took one and passed the bag along to the other jurors. "Now let's vote."

While the jury was voting, Macy sat alone in the holding cell, slowly rocking on the concrete bench and watching TV. A news reporter had located Macy's mother in another city and was asking her questions. Macy almost didn't recognize her. It had been a long time since he had seen her. She looked heavier to Macy, and her hair was a different color than he remembered from years ago. She was sitting on the front step of her house.

"What was Macy like when he was a boy?" the reporter asked.

Macy's mother looked into the TV camera and tugged on her ponytail to straighten her hair. "He was always getting into trouble," she said. "Some kids are just born bad. God knows how hard I tried to raise him right."

"What do you think the court should do with him?" the reporter asked.

"I don't really have an opinion on that," Macy's mother said.

Then Macy was led back to the courtroom to hear his sentence.

Author's Note

Shooting Monarchs is a work of fiction. The characters are imaginary, but each reminds me of someone I have known. Grandma Driscoll was inspired by my wife's grandmother, a real-life pioneer who moved to Arizona before it became a state. She grew up on a ranch, went to the university in Tucson, became a teacher, but never learned to cook. Going to Grandma's for dinner meant going to a nearby restaurant. At the end of dinner she always said the same thing: "I have a special dessert for you back at my house." Everyone knew what that meant—"gold nuggets," a simple dessert that required no cooking. Grandma dispensed the gold nuggets as if they were as valuable as their name. Then, when she turned away, the nuggets quickly disappeared into pockets, purses, and napkins. Grandma is gone, but to this day many of the "rocks" in Arizona are actually her discarded desserts.

Edie and Eddie remind me of my sister and her husband. She's a nurse and he's a police officer in New York City. Like Eddie, my brother-in-law risks his life every time he puts on the uniform. Eddie's teacher, Mr. Rappaport, is like the thousands of educators who will never know the profound, positive influence they have had on their students.

Many years ago I knew someone, like Danny, who suffered from scoliosis, a fairly common side-to-side curve of the spine. For reasons I'll never understand, he was ridiculed, unmercifully, by a person similar to Chad

Peterson. Most cases of scoliosis are mild and require no medical intervention. Serious cases, like Danny's, can usually be controlled with early detection.

The events involving Maria Hernandez and Leah Hoffman were inspired by a real girl who went for a jog and never came home. Teenage girls should not jog alone. The man who killed her was never caught. I imagine he was like Macy.

According to the National Center for Missing and Exploited Children (NCMEC), more than 3,200 children were abducted by strangers in 2001. The average victim of abduction and murder is a "low risk," "normal" girl from a stable family and middle-class neighborhood. NCMEC provides basic safety tips for girls at www.ncmec.org.